Unexpected TWIST

Previous books in the Go-for-Gold Gymnasts series

Winning Team

Balancing Act

Reaching High

Unexpected TWIST

by DOMINIQUE MOCEANU
and ALICIA THOMPSON

Disney • Hyperion Books
New York

Printed in the United States of America
First Edition
10 9 8 7 6 5 4 3 2 1
V475-2873-0 12131

Library of Congress Cataloging-in-Publication Data
Moceanu, Dominique, 1981–
Go-for-gold gymnasts: unexpected twist / by Dominique Moceanu and Alicia Thompson.—1st ed.
p. cm.—(The go-for-gold gymnasts; bk. 4)
Summary: Christina, the Texas Twister hoping to be the first Mexican-American Junior Elite all-around champion at the American Invitational, is side-lined during practice when her vault routine ends with a sharp pain in her ankle.
ISBN 978-1-4231-3658-3 (alk. paper)
[1. Gymnastics—Fiction. 2. Competition (Psychology)—Fiction. 3. Mexican Americans—Fiction. 4. Family life—Texas—Fiction. 5. Houston (Tex.)—Fiction.] I. Thompson, Alicia, 1984– II. Title.
PZ7.M71278Gou 2012
[Fic]—dc23

Designed by Tyler Nevins
Text is set in 13 point Minion Pro.

Visit www.disneyhyperionbooks.com

To all of you who wonder why life doesn't
always turn out the way you had planned:
may you recognize that the unforeseen challenges
of life take us to peaks well beyond our mind's eye.
—D. M.

For Kara
—A. T.

One

"Wow, what a fantastic question," I said. "Naturally, it's a total honor to be the first Mexican American Olympic all-around champion."

I sat at my vanity, pretending that the hairbrush in my hand was a microphone and that my reflection was a television commentator, interviewing me after the biggest triumph of my career. If only I could *pronounce* the biggest triumph of my career. Right now, it was coming off sounding like gibberish.

A publicity coach my mom hired once had taught me about enunciation. She'd even made me repeat the word *enunciation* over and over to practice it. So, I tried to say each word slower this time, really emphasizing every syllable. The last thing I wanted to do after sweeping every single event at the Olympics was to mess up the words *Olympic all-around champion.*

"Mexican American," I said, hitting every consonant like it was a hip-hop beat. "Mexican American. Olympic all-around champion."

The door to my bedroom opened, and I jumped, the hairbrush slipping out of my hand. My mother poked her head in.

I hoped she hadn't heard me talking to myself. I would have died of embarrassment.

If she'd heard me, though, her face didn't give anything away. "It's late," she said. "You need to get to bed."

It was only nine thirty. At school, kids were always talking about this one dance competition show that I was dying to watch, but it went until eleven. Because of my crazy early training at Texas Twisters, that was past my bedtime.

"Don't you knock?" I muttered.

My mother chose not to answer that question, instead crossing the room until she was standing behind me. "Let me get the back," she said, picking up the brush. With smooth, even strokes, she started brushing my hair.

I'd always had long hair. It was black and glossy and hung in waves almost to my waist, weighed down at the bottom by soft curls. My mom had the same hair. She went to the salon twice a month to get some serum put on it that would keep it shiny. I had the take-home version of the same product, and if I forgot to apply it before a big competition, all my mom had to say was, "Shine!" and I would remember. One time, my teammates overheard her saying it and assumed she was telling me I needed to stand out in my routines. Which, of course, she did also remind me about all the time.

"Maybe I could skip ballet tomorrow," I said.

My mother yanked the brush through one particularly troublesome knot at the nape of my neck, and I winced.

"You always go to ballet on Sunday mornings," she said.

"Yeah, but I also go to ballet every week with the other girls and work on my dance moves then. So it's not like it would kill me to miss a day." I didn't say what I really wanted to, which was that it would be awesome to sleep in just once. During the school week, I woke up at five thirty to be at the gym by six thirty. On Saturdays, I had to be at the gym by eight. Sunday was my only day without any gymnastics practice, but because of these extra ballet lessons, I had to be at the studio by eight, which meant I never got to sleep in.

But I knew if I had said this to my mother, she would have gotten those little frown lines in the middle of her forehead and said something about how you had to work hard if you wanted results.

She didn't speak until she was finished; the brush glided through my hair like a swan through water. "You love ballet," she said at last.

I'd actually started out as a dancer, not a gymnast. But somewhere in elementary school, I'd begun spending more time on learning a punch front than on learning a passé, and started trading recitals for competitions. It had happened really fast, like, I blinked, and—surprise!—I was a gymnast.

My mother leaned down to kiss my forehead. Her lips were cool. "Get some sleep," she said.

I waited until I heard the door click shut behind her and the soft padding of her feet on the wood floor, and then I lifted the hairbrush back to my mouth to continue my fake interview. "I love ballet,"

I said, pasting a smile on my face. I imagined the interviewer nodding, remarking that I certainly had beautiful lines, and that that must have been the effect of all that extra training. I humbly bowed my head, acknowledging the imagined compliment but not agreeing with it outright.

"I'm lucky to be competing here at the Olympics with the best gymnasts in the world," I said. That was another thing my publicity coach had suggested: always make sure you give credit to others, while still not letting the interviewer forget that you're in an elite group of athletes.

Still, I would have to work on that answer. As if luck had anything to do with gymnastics. It wasn't luck that made me finally learn the tucked full-in I'd been trying forever to get on floor. It was the hours and hours of repetition, performing the skill into a foam pit, on mats, with a spot . . . getting advice from my coaches, Cheng and Mo, and even from my teammates. It also wasn't luck that made me earn a spot on the National team. It was years of waking up early and training before school, after school, on the weekends. It was my parents paying thousands of dollars for me to work out at one of the best gyms in the country. It was me, standing at the end of the vault runway in the biggest competition of my life, launching myself into the air and delivering a solid landing that gave me a score high enough to qualify as part of that National team.

Yeah, so saying I was "lucky" to be competing was like saying I was lucky to be chosen as a contestant on a game show, or to win a prize from of a cereal box. Making a face in the mirror, I let the hairbrush fall from my hand; it clattered on the glass top of the vanity.

It took only a few seconds for my mother to hear me and return, opening the door. "What's wrong?" she asked. "Why aren't you in bed?"

"I was just going."

My mom was still staring at me, but it was like she couldn't actually see me, or wasn't really looking. I wondered what she did after I went to sleep. My dad was this insanely busy cardiologist who was always being asked to speak at conferences and stuff, so most of the time it was only me and my mom at home. When I was awake, she was shuttling me to practices and cooking my meals and helping me with my homework. So when I was asleep, did she crash out and watch TV? Did she call one of her friends and complain about all of the things she had to cram into her day?

She gave me one final look, and I climbed under the covers to show her I was serious. She wished me good night one more time, switching off the light as she left the room.

Of all the ways that my mother could have used the quiet hours before bed to relax, I thought I knew what she probably did. I could imagine her pulling up gymnastics routines on the internet, watching them carefully for crowd-pleasing skills I could use myself, or opponents' moves that I would need to be wary of. She would prepare my chicken salad for lunch the next day, and put my ice packs in the freezer so I could use them after practice.

It wasn't luck that was going to get me to the Olympics, and my mother knew that better than anyone. Better, maybe, than I did.

Usually, I was one of the girls who could show everyone else in Mademoiselle Colette's ballet class how it was done.

If that sounds like bragging, it's totally not supposed to. All the girls I practiced with were, like, eight years old. The girls my age were better than me, because ballet was their thing, the same way gymnastics was mine. So it was only natural that I would completely own all of the third graders in my class with my awesome turnout and flexibility.

Okay, maybe *that's* bragging.

That morning, though, I felt off. Mademoiselle Colette tapped me on the shoulder twice to remind me about my posture, which was usually so perfect that I could balance a book on my head, the way they taught at those old-fashioned charm schools. But it was hard to concentrate on my posture when my foot was throbbing. There was a dull pain I'd been feeling lately in my heel whenever I did really hard tumbling or flexed my feet a lot . . . so, pretty much all the time.

Mademoiselle Colette passed by again, frowning at me. "Toes out," she said. "And bend—yes, like that."

I sank down in a deep plié, and had to bite my tongue to stop the small moan of pain that almost escaped my lips. But apparently the pain was written all over my face, because Mademoiselle Colette plucked the pencil from behind her ear, in a gesture she made when she was making a note of something, even though she didn't have a notebook to write anything down in.

"You are hurt?"

I shook my head. "My ankle's been a little touchy," I said, "but it's fine." I lowered myself into another plié to show her that I meant what I said, and this time, when I bit my tongue I could taste blood.

She nodded, satisfied for the time being, and moved on. As soon as her back was to me, I let my posture sag again. The weird thing was that it *wasn't* my ankle—not exactly. I'd rolled my ankle enough times to know the soreness that could result for a few days afterward, but that was not what this pain felt like.

Mademoiselle Colette might have been easy to fool, but unfortunately, my mother had eyes like a hawk. One time, I'd swiped some icing off my cousin's *quinceañera* cake, and even though I knew I'd licked all of the evidence off my fingers, somehow my mom still figured it out. Now, I felt her presence in the doorway of the classroom before she even entered, watching me go through the last series of exercises. After ballet class let out, she barely let me grab my bag before she was all over me.

"Usually you're so graceful," she said. "But today you looked like a wooden stick."

Gee, thanks, Mom. "I had an off day," I said. I wanted to add, *So what?* I worked out seven days a week. She should try being perfect three hundred sixty-three days out of the year.

"Do you need to loosen up?" she asked. "Maybe go to Ivana again?"

Ivana was a masseuse who I'd been to several times before, mostly during competition season. Her office had such a strong smell of eucalyptus that it made my nostrils burn, but she did have a knack for smoothing out the knots in my back.

"Is it practicing with those little girls?" my mom pressed. "I don't like that you always have to show them how to do the moves. It seems like, if Mademoiselle Colette wanted an assistant, she should hire one, instead of making *you* spend *your* dance time teaching them."

Even though it was kind of weird to dance alongside kids who were still in elementary school, I actually kind of liked getting to be the teacher for a while. I was about to open my mouth and tell my mother so, when she cut me off.

"Then again, you weren't being asked to assist

today," she said, with a disdainful tone as she said the word *today,* as if there was no measuring stick in the world to gauge just how badly I'd done. "Should I ask Mademoiselle Colette if she could give private lessons? Maybe that's the answer."

"I don't need private lessons," I muttered.

Sometimes, I had to remind myself to be grateful for everything I had in my life. My teammates sure didn't have a masseuse on call; my best friend Noelle was lucky if she had the money to sit in one of those massaging chairs at the mall. During the past summer, she almost didn't make it to Junior Nationals because her parents could barely afford it. Meanwhile, I had practice equipment in our basement and custom leotards and extra lessons, because my dad made a boatload of money every year. For us, those things weren't that big a deal, and I had to stop to remind myself that they *were* a big deal for a lot of people. There were people who would have killed to be in my position.

My mom used her clicker to unlock the doors as we reached the SUV. I climbed into the front seat, and she glanced over at me as she started the car.

"I'll call Ivana for an appointment," she said.

I smiled. It *had* been a really hard day, and my

body was feeling achy and tired. A massage was just what I needed.

"She can focus on your legs especially," my mom added. "Maybe she can loosen you up so that ring leap on the floor is more elegant."

I felt the smile fade from my face, but my mother was already concentrating on backing out of the parking space, so she didn't notice. I was lucky, I reminded myself again. Lucky, lucky, lucky.

Two

There was a buzz in the air when I got to gym on Monday morning. I couldn't explain it, but it was there, almost like I could feel the gym vibrating. Normally, these early morning practices were kind of a drag; although we were all used to waking up before the earliest school bus started its route, we weren't necessarily morning people.

Or maybe that was just me. Britt, for example, often reminded me of the Energizer Bunny, and this morning she was wound up extra tight.

"What's this announcement Mo's talking about?" she asked. "Why does she always have to tease us like this? Why, why, why?"

Did I mention that I kind of find the Energizer Bunny annoying? Who wouldn't?

"I might have an idea," I said cryptically. Mostly, I said this to shut Britt up. Also, in case one of the other girls actually knew something, I wanted to avoid looking like I was out of the loop.

Besides, it was totally plausible that I might have had some inside information. If anyone knew the skinny on what happened in the gym, it would be my mom. She worked at the front desk several days a week, and when she wasn't there, she could always be found in the viewing section, watching me with a critical gaze. If there had been some huge announcement, it was very possible she would know what it was about. But then, why wouldn't she have told me?

Jessie and Noelle had been chatting over by the water fountain, but now they came up to join us. "Are you talking about the announcement?" Jessie asked. "All that Mo will say is that we should do our stretches like normal and then she'll fill us in."

Britt snorted. She was cute with her little white-blond ponytail and bright blue eyes (although she would have killed me if she heard me call her cute), but that noise reminded me of a piglet. "Like I care about touching my toes right now," she said. "Christina has a clue about what's going on, though. I told you she would."

All eyes were now on me, including Noelle's earnest brown ones. "Is that true?" she asked. "Can you at least give us a hint?"

I thought about stretching the lie out further, but I couldn't do that to Noelle.

I knew from our years of friendship that she could be pretty gullible and took things very seriously. One summer after we'd first met, I told her that swallowing watermelon seeds would make a whole watermelon grow in your stomach. I hadn't said it to be mean; I hadn't thought she'd believe me. To this day, she still spits out all the seeds, even though I've explained to her a hundred times that I was joking.

"I was kidding," I said again now. "I'm as clueless as you guys. What's going on? What announcement are you talking about?"

"Mo wouldn't reveal any juicy details," Britt said, "and yet she expects us to go warm up like it's any other day. This is torture."

We all glanced over at Mo, who was standing

by the front desk rifling through a stack of papers as though nothing unusual was going on. My mother was there, too, on the telephone, probably answering some phone call about tumbling lessons for tots, and she was also acting completely cool. I doubted that she was in on whatever Mo was cooking up. My mom's not exactly known for keeping secrets or for subtlety, especially when it comes to my gymnastics. And if she had been aware of a big announcement this morning, no way would she have let me be late, even if I'd been running around trying to find my gym bag. She'd sooner have restocked my entire gym bag from the pro shop than let me miss something like this.

Mo looked over in our direction, so we all tried to pretend we hadn't been staring. I turned my head to face the row of beams, as though I were contemplating which one I wanted to practice on later. Jessie picked at some imaginary dirt under her fingernails, and Britt kept tightening her ponytail, which was already as tight as it could be.

"We better start stretching," Noelle said. "The sooner we finish, the sooner we can hear this big announcement."

It was hard to argue with that, so the four of us

started our stretching routine with an enthusiasm we rarely showed in the morning. We attacked our straddle positions ruthlessly, as though there were going to be punishment for anything less than a perfect one-hundred-and-eighty-degree split. We bent forward until our noses touched the floor. There was a slight twinge in my heel when I pointed my toes, but I barely even noticed.

When we had finally completed our exercises, we all lined up on the mat the way Mo liked us to do when she had something to tell us. Usually, we did this at the start of competition season, when Mo would tell each of us how our practices were going to change to fit our individual training for upcoming meets. We'd also lined up this way a few other times, like when Mo hired a nutritionist to talk to us about our diets or when a representative from USA Gymnastics came to discuss the stipend we would earn as part of the National team.

I could almost hear each girl holding her breath when Mo stood in front of us at last. There was the tiniest smile at the corner of Mo's mouth, as though she had picked up on the fever pitch of our anticipation and found it amusing.

Mo used to be a gymnast herself, back in her

native China, and she wasn't much taller than us. In spite of that, she commanded our total respect. Even though I wanted to scream, "Tell us, already!" and Britt was practically jumping out of her skin, we stayed quiet until Mo spoke.

"I receive exciting news today," she said. "You have all heard of American Invitational, yes?"

We all nodded. The American Invitational was one of the biggest international competitions that our country hosted, which attracted the very best American gymnasts and some of the top gymnasts from other countries, too.

"As you know, competition is for Senior Elite girls only," Mo continued. "No Juniors. So you can't go."

It was true that we wouldn't be allowed to *compete* until we were fifteen, but that didn't mean we couldn't attend the meet as fans up in the stands. I was starting to get the feeling that maybe that was what this was about. We'd gone on a team trip to see a competition before, a couple years ago, when the Nationals were held in Fort Worth. But this would be even better, because we'd get to see girls from all over the world.

"But this year is Olympic year," Mo said, "and

they change the rule. Now, they are adding Junior level of competition."

Wait a second. Had Mo said what I thought she'd said? Was there a possibility that we would be going to the American Invitational not as spectators, but as . . .

Mo nodded, as though she could hear the whir of all of our thoughts. "That's right," she said, "and they invite every one of you to compete."

She let that sink in for only a moment, but it was enough time for me to glance at Noelle and grin. I knew that the sparkle in her eyes was probably reflected in mine. The American Invitational! This was even bigger than the USA vs. the World event that we'd competed at just a month before, since that had been more of an exhibition event for us Juniors. We were supposed to do a couple of routines, show what we could do, see some sights, and then go home.

This was a real competition, and one of us had the chance to be the first Junior all-around champion ever.

There was only that brief moment of excitement, though, and then Mo made sure to bring us back down to earth. She was good at that. "We don't waste time," she said. "So, go, join Cheng at the bars."

I loved the bars. I felt so tall, somehow, when I circled around and around those bars, even though obviously that was one event where it paid to be shorter. The shorter you were, the more room you had to move between the bars, which meant you could execute more tricks and not worry as much about hitting your feet on one bar while you swung around the other. But even so, there was something about the stretched-out way my body felt, from the tips of my fingers to the point of my toes, that felt really awesome.

We did a few exercises before building up to our big skills. One of my favorite elements in my routine was a Pak salto, where I let go of the high bar, did a complete backflip in a layout position, and then grabbed the low bar. For a split second while I was between the bars, it felt like I was flying.

On my first Pak salto in practice, I caught the low bar solidly, chalk puffing out from underneath my fingers. I opened my legs into a straddle position, my toes just skimming the blue mat before I jumped down. Eagerly, I looked to Cheng for feedback—I knew I'd done well.

"Don't arch back," was all he said, giving me

a dismissive nod before motioning to the next girl to go.

I'd thought my body position was pretty good, but apparently not. My face must've shown how discouraged I felt, because Mo gave me a brief pat on the shoulder.

"Over the next two month, we will all work harder than we ever have before," she said, and I understood. I'd been good, but good wasn't good enough. I would need to be great.

It would all be worth it in four years, when I gave that interview after winning Olympic gold. "Yes," I would say, "it really did all start with becoming the first Junior American Invitational champion. That's when I felt like, this is it. This is what I was born to do."

That night, I convinced my mother to let Noelle sleep over, even though we had early morning practice and school the next day. I told her that we had to work on an English project together, which was partly true, and also that we were so excited about the American Invitational that we had to talk about it, which was all true.

"I bet that *Flip for Gymnastics* will profile the

Junior champion at the Invitational," Noelle said. We were sitting on my bed, flicking through past issues of that magazine and admiring the perfect toe point and powerful tumbling in the pictures. I knew from going to Jessie's house that she had a subscription to the magazine, too, but the posters in all of hers had been ripped out, the jagged edges left near the centerfold reminding her to glance up at her walls at huge pictures of some of the greatest gymnasts ever. My posters, on the other hand, were still inside, completely intact. My mother didn't like me to hang anything other than framed art on the walls, because she thought posters were tacky.

"They'd better," I said. "I mean, everyone will care about the Senior champion who might go to the Olympics this year, but people will also be dying to know more about up-and-coming talent like us."

Of course, only one of us could be that all-around champion . . . and it might be neither of us. But Noelle and I didn't talk about that, even though it must have been on her mind, too.

Noelle set the magazine down on my purple comforter, dropping her voice as though confessing a big secret. "When it was my turn to go to the library today," she said, "I spent most of my time looking up the American Invitational on the computer."

"Me, too!" I said. Technically, the assignment we were supposed to be working on in Ms. Rine's English class was an essay about where we saw ourselves in five years, so looking up the Invitational wasn't even really cheating. I saw myself in gymnastics, so doing an internet search for the American Invitational was like research.

"It's in New Orleans this year," Noelle said. "That's only eight hours away if we drive. Do you think we'll all carpool together?"

"Wow," I said, "you *did* spend some time on this. I was too busy trying to watch videos of past competitions to see how big the crowd is and to check where this year's competition would be held."

"I think Jessie has this year's Invitational on her DVR," Noelle said. "We could probably go over there and watch it."

There was a brief rap at the door, and then my mother peeked in. "Are you working on your English homework?"

I held up the magazine; it was an issue from four years ago that had the Olympic champion on the cover. "We're doing research," I said, in an almost exact echo of what I'd told Ms. Rine about my library visit earlier that day. "The essay has to be about where we see ourselves in five years, so we're looking at gymnastics magazines for ideas."

My mom chuckled. "That's a no-brainer," she said. "In five years, you'll probably be on tour with other superstars, showing off your gold medals on every major talk show. You'll be that girl on the cover."

She nodded toward Noelle. "You, too, of course," she said. I could tell she meant it—she loved Noelle and thought she was an amazing gymnast—but I knew she also expected me to do a little bit better than everyone else. Sure, Noelle could win a gold medal, but I'd win more. I'd win the all-around, the one that counted the most because it meant you were the best gymnast overall.

And if I didn't—if Noelle or Britt or Jessie won, or (ugh) some other random gymnast—well, then, my mom might just adopt her.

Just kidding. Or maybe not.

"Do you need anything?" my mom asked. "I can make you some ice-cream sandwiches with graham crackers and Cool Whip."

I was about to turn her down—not because I don't love sweet stuff, but because I kind of wanted her to go away so Noelle and I could hang out—but Noelle's eyes lit up. "I would love some!"

Once my mom had left, Noelle sighed. "Your mom is so nice," she said.

"I guess."

"What do you mean, you *guess*?"

I realized that that had probably sounded bad, so I hurried to explain myself. It was true that my mother was very nice—she did everything for me, and she would do almost anything for my teammates, too. It's just that sometimes I felt like I needed a break.

"I guess I take it for granted," I said, forcing a smile. "You're right; she's supernice."

We went back to looking through magazines until my mom returned with our treats. "You two need to wrap it up in the next half hour," she said. "I'll make omelets in the morning, but only if you aren't impossible to get up. And it *is* a school night."

"We *know*," I said, speaking through a mouthful of graham cracker and Cool Whip. It was probably a good thing that my words came out as a garbled mess, because if my mom had heard me take that tone in front of a guest, the party would've been shut down right then. Instead, she closed the door behind her, leaving Noelle and me to snack.

"We should probably get to work," Noelle said. "I wanted to have at least an outline done so I could show it to Ms. Rine tomorrow."

That was Noelle. Always going above and beyond, doing eighteen times the work she needed to, or preparing way in advance. I had no clue how she found the time, but I also didn't understand why she would want to spend so much energy on school. Even if I hadn't had gymnastics, I still wouldn't have devoted myself to something as boring as English.

For example, one of our assignments had been to write a report about how C. S. Lewis describes Mr. Tumnus's house in his book *The Lion, the Witch and the Wardrobe*. Ms. Rine had made us write down some of the actual words he used, and we weren't allowed to watch the movie and describe it that way. But if there was a movie already, then why bother with the book?

"What's to outline?" I said. "In five years, you'll be on talk shows and stuff, telling the host about how you won Olympic gold. We all will."

Noelle bit her lip. "We'll have to make sure that our essays sound different," she said. "Since we have practically the same goals, Ms. Rine might think we copied or something."

"I'm not going to copy," I protested hotly. I may not have liked English, but that didn't mean I was a cheater.

"I didn't say you were," Noelle said. She ripped out some sheets of paper from her notebook, taking that paper for herself and letting me use the actual notebook. "Let's freewrite for five minutes, like Ms. Rine makes us do. Starting . . . now."

Noelle began scribbling, stopping only to place a book under the pages to make it easier to write. She was like that in class, too—when Ms. Rine made us freewrite about various topics at the start of class, Noelle had no trouble filling an entire page with her thoughts about whether animal testing was ever justified, or what five historical figures she'd invite to a dinner party and why.

I used to really like writing—not necessarily for school, but as a way to release some of my feelings. I would write little poems that weren't any good but were another way for me to reflect on things in my life. I even used to keep a diary, where I laid out all my thoughts and fears and hopes and worries. But my mom was always reading it, sneaking peeks when she said she was just putting my clothes away in my drawer, so I stopped keeping it.

Now, in school, I hated freewrite time. My mind wandered, and sometimes I couldn't think of anything interesting to say. I didn't like the idea of testing on animals, or I thought I'd like to have dinner with Amelia Earhart, but that was it. There was nothing else to add.

But I didn't want Noelle to think I didn't listen to her, so I put pen to paper and forced myself to come up with some words.

In five years, I hope to . . .

Maybe that sounded too doubtful. Maybe, I thought, I should write it as though I knew what was going to happen, as though I had a crystal ball to see into the future.

In five years, I will be a famous gymnast. I will have won the all-around gold at the Olympics, and everyone will want to hear me talk about my amazing experiences. I will tell them all of the details, like . . .

I tapped my pen against the wire binding of the notebook until Noelle glanced at me; I stopped.

What *were* the details? That was the hard part. But the essay had to be at least three pages long, typed, so I had to come up with something.

Noelle already had the entire front of a page covered, and was flipping it over to start on the back.

Ms. Rine always wanted us to use "sensory" details, such as how things tasted or smelled or what they looked like. So, I tried to think of some of those.

I will tell them all of the details, like what victory tastes like and the smell of the stadium and what the scoreboard looks like.

I felt as if I was using the word *like* too much. Plus, they weren't really interesting details. I was just listing things. I tore my paper out of the notebook, crumpled it into a ball, and threw it on the floor.

"We can stop if you want," Noelle said, her gaze on the discarded piece of paper. I knew if I didn't pick it up, she would, because she'd be worried about getting in trouble with my mom, who liked me to keep my room immaculate. So I bent down and scooped it back up, flattening it out in front of me.

"I'm not even wearing a watch," Noelle admitted. "I don't know why I said we'd do it for five minutes when I have no idea what time it is."

"It's not a big deal," I said. "I just need to think about it more. What did you write?"

She hesitated for a second, and I rolled my eyes. "I am *not* going to copy you, I promise," I said. "When have I ever done that?"

"I'm not saying you would *mean* to," she said, then cleared her throat. Sitting up straight, she held the paper in front of her as if she was about to present some groundbreaking research.

"In five years, I will be eighteen years old," Noelle read. *"I see myself on a tour with Olympic champions traveling the country, performing in front of crowds of thousands of people. When I'm introduced before my first routine, the announcer says, 'And now, Olympic all-around gold-medalist Noelle Onesti!' Then I come out, waving to the crowd, and they cheer louder than for anyone else."*

Her gaze flickered toward me for a second, as though she were checking my reaction to that part. I smiled to let her know that it was okay. We all wanted to win, but that didn't mean we wouldn't be happy if any one of us did well.

Noelle continued, *"The lights are hot and bright overhead as I take my position on the floor. Then the music starts up, that song 'Gir—'"* She broke off, shooting me a sheepish look. *"And I flip and dance across the floor as the crowd claps along to the music."*

"What song?" I prompted. It was obvious that Noelle was embarrassed about it, and that was too good an opportunity to pass up. No way was I letting her off the hook.

She held her paper up to her face for a moment, trying to hide a blush. "'Girls Just Want to Have Fun,'" she said. "I know it's cheesy, but it's so catchy! And I could picture the exact moves I would do, and the pink leotard I would wear. . . ."

"Oh," I said. That wasn't really embarrassing at all. "No, that song rocks. It would make an awesome routine."

Those details were exactly the kind I needed for *my* essay. Noelle could imagine the sounds of the crowd and her floor music, the feel of the hot lights. She probably could picture every single groove in her Olympic gold medal. But for whatever reason, those sorts of ideas didn't come easily to me. Maybe I was just a horrible writer.

"Let's go to bed," I said abruptly, shoving the notebook off my lap. "Any second now, my mom will come in here, and she'll be mad if we don't have the lights off."

Noelle looked a little surprised. I never went to bed before my mother made her last call—if I could, I loved to push it just a half hour more—or an hour, or two hours. I always lived in hope that my mom might forget my bedtime just once and let me stay up. I also lived in hope that one Sunday morning she might forget about ballet practice and accidentally let me sleep in. Obviously, neither of these things had happened yet.

Noelle and I brushed our teeth together in silence, changed into our pajamas, and climbed into my large canopy bed. I was lying there in the dark, wondering whether she was asleep already, when I heard her voice.

"Christina?"

I loved Noelle, but I wasn't sure if I felt up to talking. So I uttered a tired-sounding "Mmmhmm?"

"The crowd will cheer loudly for you, too," she said. "The way I see us in five years, the crowd will cheer when they announce your name, too. I just wanted you to know that."

"Thanks," I said. But I lay awake long after my mother had come to check on us, and wondered why I couldn't have the same vision as Noelle. I was excited about the American Invitational, of course. And I could spend hours in front of my mirror rehearsing acceptance speeches and answers to interview questions. But when it came time to picture the actual scene, the stuck dismount that would seal my gold medal or the standing ovation I would receive for a flawless routine, the image seemed a little out of focus.

Three

Jump backward, half twist, tuck, *bam*. Backward, half twist, tuck, *bam*. I was on my tenth Arabian of morning practice so far, and I could feel myself improving every time my feet hit the mat.

I'd been working on this skill forever. Or at least, that's how it seemed. First, I'd done drills on the floor to get used to the feeling of it. In an Arabian, you jump up like you're going to do a backflip, but then at peak height, you twist and flip forward instead. Eventually, I was going to include a double-tucked Arabian in my floor routine, which would add a ton of difficulty to my score, but for now, I was still working on a single flip.

It was harder than I'd thought to adjust my body to the skill. That's why the drills on the floor had been important—I would jump up and twist to roll onto a stack of mats behind me. At first, my instinct had been to land and then roll, but the whole point of the skill is to twist and flip simultaneously, not to twist first and then flip later. Even though I understood how necessary the drills had been, they were still annoying and felt like they lasted a billion years.

After that, the next step was to do the skill on the Tumbl Trak before finally performing it on the actual floor, which was what I was doing now. Every time I hit the mat—*bam*—it reverberated in my heel.

Cheng nodded when I completed my fifteenth pass, letting me know that I was doing a good job. Normally, even that hint of praise was enough to keep me glowing for the rest of practice, but instead I felt a bit distracted.

"That was awesome," Britt said from one of the beams. She was supposed to be working on her standing full twist with Mo, but had stopped to watch me for a moment. That would have been Mo's cue to direct Britt to stay on task, but she was watching me, too.

"You ready for double Arabian," she said. "Maybe for Invitational."

I felt my heart almost leap out of my chest and then crash down again. The prospect of doing this same skill but with more height and with twice the flips was exciting, but it was also terrifying. It had taken me so long to master this skill; how was I going to learn an even more difficult version?

When I was trying to qualify to be an Elite gymnast, I added a piked full-in to my floor routine to boost my score. Now, I could do a hundred of those and land ninety-nine, but it had taken me a long time to learn how to do it. And while that skill involved similar elements to the ones in the Arabian—twisting and flipping—it was harder to twist to face forward and to land blindly, with no sight of the mat until right before your feet hit. It was going to be tough to get that skill perfect in time for the Invitational.

All of us were working on some new trick for this Invitational, even if it was only honing a skill we'd been practicing for a while but had never competed. That was the case with Britt, who was trying to perfect her standing back full on the beam in time. Noelle had a new mount on beam she'd just unveiled at Nationals, but now she was also adding a complicated leap series to her floor routine. Jessie was upping the level of difficulty on her vault with an extra half twist.

I glanced over at my mom, who was sitting in the parents' viewing section, and for some reason I had this weird sense of déjà vu. I'd been training alongside Noelle and Jessie for three years, and with Britt for almost a year. I remembered when Britt had tried that standing back full without a spot, and how mad Mo had been, because she could've really hurt herself. I remembered when Jessie had been scared to twist at all after hitting the vaulting table, much less do more than one rotation in the air.

Without even thinking about it, I lifted my hand to wave at my mom, the way I'd done when I was younger. She had a notebook in her lap, which from a distance made it look like she was playing Sudoku or something, but I knew she was taking notes so we could talk about them later. She jotted down things like what Mo told me to work on, and how many reps I did of each skill. Instead of waving back, she drew her brows together, like she was trying to figure out if anything was wrong. She started to stand up, but then I turned away.

"Christina?" Mo's voice snapped me back to attention. "You ready?"

It took me a second to remember that she'd been talking about that double Arabian I could add to my routine. I nodded, hoping I looked confident. I tried to visualize myself doing the skill, using all the sensory detail Ms. Rine would want in my essay. *My feet are dry and white from the chalk covering the soles, and I leave footprints on the blue carpet as I run across the floor. I can feel the burn in my calf muscles as I launch into my round-off to a back handspring, and then . . .*

I couldn't picture landing the actual double Arabian, though. No matter how many times I tried to see it, it was like a film that had been cut off before the ending.

I knew my mom was still watching me, and I could almost feel her willing me to answer Mo more enthusiastically than with a simple nod. I could hear her berating me in the car, telling me that Mo was giving me a huge opportunity to stand out, and instead all I'd done was fade into the background.

So I forced a huge smile, allowing a hint of arrogance into my voice. "Oh, yeah," I said. "I'm ready to rock it."

* * *

Ms. Rine stood in front of our English class droning on about *Great Expectations*, and I found myself daydreaming about my double Arabian and the Invitational, and basically everything but Pip and his benefactor.

Ms. Rine's classroom had posters covering every inch of the walls. There was a long yellow banner that said, WHAT'S RIGHT ISN'T ALWAYS POPULAR. WHAT'S POPULAR ISN'T ALWAYS RIGHT. There was a motivational poster with the word *Leadership* on it and a picture of a bald eagle, even though I wasn't totally sure what the two had to do with each other. And then there was one that had a quote from Audrey Hepburn: NOTHING IS IMPOSSIBLE, THE WORD ITSELF SAYS, "I'M POSSIBLE!"

I bet Audrey Hepburn never did a double Arabian in her life.

"Christina?" Ms. Rine's voice cut into my thoughts.

I blinked. "Yes?"

"I asked you about the significance of the title," Ms. Rine said patiently.

I glanced at Noelle, hoping she could help me, but she was staring at me with the same blank, waiting expression that Ms. Rine had. "Title?" I repeated.

Ms. Rine took her glasses off and wiped them with the hem of her shirt. I noticed that she did this a lot when she wanted to pause or think about something. Right now, I wished I had an action that I could do to delay this conversation, because the silence was lasting a bit too long, and it was becoming more and more obvious that I had no clue what Ms. Rine was talking about.

"*Great Expectations,*" she said, adding, "the book we've been reading for the last month."

There was a movie for this one that I hadn't watched yet, although Ms. Rine had cautioned us not to rely on it, because apparently it was a "modern adaptation," whatever that meant. All I knew from the poster for the movie was that the leading guy looked cute, and the leading lady was that blond woman who was in everything and talked with a British accent even though she wasn't British. When I suggested to my mom that we rent it, she'd made a weird choking sound and moved me toward the animated movies.

"Pip has great expectations?" I guessed. At least I got the name of the main character right. It was a weird name, so it wasn't hard to remember.

"Yes," Ms. Rine said. I felt a moment of relief. I glanced at Noelle, who smiled at me. Off the hook.

"But expectations of what?" Ms. Rine prompted. "And how do these play out throughout the story?"

I was completely stuck. We had a test on the book coming in a few weeks, right before the winter holidays, and I'd fully intended to read it before then. But for now, I wasn't entirely sure how to answer Ms. Rine's question, so I mumbled that I didn't know, and sank further in my seat.

Although she looked disappointed, Ms. Rine didn't push it. Instead, she turned to address the whole class. "After Pip gets the money, he has tremendous expectations for his future. He wants to be famous, he wants to marry Estella, and he becomes almost arrogant about the fact that he will achieve these things. Do you think it served him well to set his sights so high? Or do you think he should've been more realistic, more humble?"

Oh, no. Not another question. I waited for her to direct it toward me, since she seemed to love picking on me, but just then, the bell rang. For once, I had been paying such close attention to her that I hadn't even noticed that class was wrapping up. I had to admit that it was usually the opposite.

"Think about that for your homework tonight," Ms. Rine said, "in addition to answering the questions on page forty-five of your textbook about characterization. I'll see you tomorrow!"

I scooped up my books, glad to get out from underneath her watchful eyes. But on my way out the door, she said my name. Busted.

"Yeah?" I said.

"Can I speak to you for a minute?"

I considered telling her that I would be late for my next class, which might have been true, but wouldn't get me out of this conversation. She'd just have offered me a hall pass or something.

Noelle looked wide-eyed, as though *she'd* been asked to stay after class. She hated getting in trouble so much that she got worried about being guilty by association. Me, I was kind of used to being in the doghouse. My mom was upset with me all the time, it seemed like, for not applying myself as much as I could in the gym or for slacking off in ballet.

So when I stood in front of Ms. Rine, my arms crossed over my chest, I wasn't that worried about being in trouble. I wanted to get this confrontation over with, so I could move on to my next class, and then go to practice and work on the stuff that really mattered.

"Have you started on your essay yet?" Ms. Rine asked me. At first I thought she meant some essay about *Great Expectations* I'd forgotten about, and I got a little freaked out. But then it occurred to me that she must have meant the one about where we saw ourselves in five years.

"Actually," I said, "I have." It was even true!

She beamed at me. "Excellent," she said. "And what have you come up with so far?"

Was she serious? She had to know I was a gymnast. Everyone in school knew about me and Noelle, because the morning announcements would sometimes include this embarrassing good luck or congratulations message if we had a competition. I think most people even knew about Britt, even though she'd been homeschooled until this year.

"Uh, gymnastics," I said. *Obviously.*

"Great," Ms. Rine said. There was a stack of papers on her desk with red numbers written at the top. I was trying so hard to see if I could read the numbers upside down and find out someone's grade that I almost missed her next question.

"So, what, specifically?" she asked.

I didn't understand why she was grilling me like this. I bet she wasn't interviewing anyone else about their essays. I mean, Noelle had the exact same goals that I did, and she was allowed to continue on to her next class, no problem.

Come to think of it, I wasn't in love with my next class, which was Social Studies. We were always having to do group projects in there. Total drag.

"The Olympics, of course," I said. "In four years, I'll be old enough to go. And then, after that, there are all kinds of tours and television appearances and stuff. Some gymnasts have even had little parts in TV shows or gone on *Dancing with the Stars* and that kind of thing, which would be cool."

"I think that's fantastic," Ms. Rine said. "You're so talented, and lucky to have such a clear sense of what you want."

Maybe that was all Ms. Rine had wanted to tell me. The last big competition, the USA vs. the World, had been televised, and they'd shown one whole routine of mine. I wondered if Ms. Rine had seen it, and wanted to let me know that she was a fan. That would have been pretty cool.

Then again, that was never how things worked

out. Like, when my mom told me that I had beautiful toe point, it was usually a setup for a lecture about why I should be taking more ballet or how I needed to live up to my potential. So, really, I wasn't surprised when Ms. Rine's compliment led to something else.

"As you write, though, I want you to remember Pip," she said. "Think about his great expectations, and keep in mind that for this essay I'm not simply interested in where you end up. I'm interested in how you plan to get there."

Ms. Rine handed me back a previous paper that had been in the stack, saying something else about the number at the top of it. But I was barely listening. I was still focused on what she'd just said. Basically, she was telling me that my goals for myself—my dream—was *too* great. She was comparing it to Pip's stupid desire to land himself this one snobby girl as his wife.

She didn't seem to get that my situation was totally different. You can't *make* someone fall in love with you or want to be with you. But I could make the Olympics happen. Otherwise, what was the point of it all?

Four

I knew I pretended to be great at every-thing, but even I acknowledged that vault wasn't my best event. There was no room for grace or creativity or interpretation in vault, though those are the things that drew me to gymnastics. It was just about power, which Jessie had, or consistency, which Noelle was good at, or fearlessness, which was totally Britt's thing.

Most of the vaults we did were Yurchenkos, in which you approached the vaulting table backward. Even though I'd been competing a Yurchenko for over a year, I still got butterflies in my stomach when I stood at the end of the runway and contemplated actually doing that kind of skill.

That afternoon at practice, it didn't help that my heel was bothering me again. Noelle noticed me wincing while we stood in line for our turn at the vault.

"Are you okay?" she asked.

It hurt just to watch Britt sprint down the runway. I felt twinges in my heel every time I heard Jessie's feet pounding the mat in a hard landing.

"I'm fine," I said. "I think I may have bruised my foot or something, that's all."

Noelle made a sympathetic face. "I hate when that happens," she said. "My mom always tells me to—"

But Cheng was motioning impatiently for Noelle to take her turn, and so she had to snap back to attention without finishing what she had to say. She didn't even take the time to brush the bottoms of her feet with chalk, to ensure maximum traction as she ran down the runway. But of course, even without it, Noelle executed a flawless Yurchenko one-and-a-half.

Once she was off the mat, Cheng waved his hand at me, making the signal to go. Unlike Noelle, I took the time to put a little more chalk on my feet—not really because they needed it, but more because it delayed my vault a bit.

But this time, it wasn't only butterflies that I felt in my stomach. It was dread, as if instead of running down the vault runway I was walking the plank. But that was silly. So I didn't love vault. I'd still done a million of them in my lifetime, and would have to do more if I wanted to make it to the Olympics. My foot hurt, but I'd practiced and competed through some kind of pain almost every day of my gymnastics career. It was the way it was.

Behind me, Jessie and Britt were debating the lyrics of some song and whether they were "your life" or "you're alive." I wanted to weigh in, because I knew the answer and it was so obvious, but I had to focus. Cheng was waiting for me, and I had to get through this vault and then get back in line so I could do it all over again. I took a deep breath.

As soon as I started running, the pain was sharp and ran all the way up my left leg. I wanted to stop, but I made myself push through, jumping into a round-off onto the springboard—*bam!*—to twisting off the vault table, once all the way around, until my feet hit the mat—*bam!* I landed squarely, my feet frozen on the blue vinyl of the mat.

Cheng clapped his hands together, which normally would have made me glow all over, since Cheng rarely shows much emotion about anything and has definitely never been that jazzed about any of my vaults before. But I couldn't enjoy it, because the pain was now like fire, a hot blue flame in my foot and the still scorching red, orange, and yellow flames traveling up my calf and shin to my knee.

I sank down onto the mat, clutching my leg. Cheng was by my side in an instant, his gentle hands on my ankle. I could tell that even he was flustered, because at first he tried to talk to me in Chinese before switching to English to ask me what hurt.

"It's fine," I tried to say, but I choked back a sob. It really hurt. I knew without Cheng's making me wiggle my toes or flex my ankle that nothing was broken. It hadn't been a sudden pain, and already it was dying down to a dull throb.

Mo had left the girls she was helping on the balance beams and was standing over us, watching the whole exchange. Noelle, Jessie, and Britt were still at the other end of the vault runway, since they knew they'd get in trouble if they came over to gawk like people do at a bad car accident, but they were inching closer, their mouths open and their eyes worried. My mom had left her position at the front desk and was coming over to check on me.

"Is everything okay?" she asked. "Christina, what is it? Are you hurt?"

"I'm fine," I said. I felt like a broken record. "I guess I landed weird or something. But everything is okay—ask Cheng."

My mom turned her gaze to him, raising her eyebrows as if to say, *Well? Is that true?*

"Nothing is broken," he said cautiously, giving my Achilles tendon a gentle squeeze. I flinched.

Mo's gaze missed nothing. "Did that hurt?"

"Only a little," I said. "I'll ice it when I get home."

"You are crying," Mo said. As if I couldn't be any *more* embarrassed, Mo had to point it out for the whole gym, who were all trying to listen and see what happened, even if they pretended they were only doing the stretches or reps they were supposed to be doing.

I couldn't think of anything to say so I decided not to say anything at all. There were tears pooling in my eyes; I didn't know if it would be more obvious to wipe them away or to let them fall, so I just looked down at my toes like I was evaluating my pedicure. We weren't allowed to wear colored polish for competitions, so my toenails were painted with clear.

Mo seemed to sense my discomfort, because she crouched down next to me. "If you crying, it not nothing," she said. "How long it feel like this?"

I shrugged, finally wiping away a tear. "A few weeks," I said. "A month. I don't know. It comes and goes."

"Why didn't you tell me about it?" my mom asked. I'd almost forgotten she was standing there. She turned to Mo. "Is it serious? Will it affect training for the Invitational?"

Mo and my mom have a pretty good relationship, since my mom works up at the front desk all the time and comes to every competition, team-building event, and fund-raiser. But now, Mo shifted her weight so her back was to my mother. It was very slight, but I noticed it, and so did my mom; I could tell by the way her face tightened.

"We do not worry about Invitational right now," Mo said. "I will give you name of doctor, and he will see what we need to do. Yes?"

I nodded, because it was all I could really do. I didn't want to go to the doctor; I was scared of what he might tell me. And I definitely didn't want to forget about the Invitational.

Noelle, Jessie, and Britt had managed to work their way over to within a yard of me, they murmured words of encouragement until Cheng finally told them to get back to practice. That was my cue to get off the mat, since it meant that there were gymnasts who needed to continue training. I headed to the locker room to grab my bag.

It was only when my mom and I were out in the cold December air, the sky a lighter blue than I was used to seeing after practice, that I remembered the lyrics I'd been going to correct Britt on. *Your life*, they said. *Your life.*

Mo had given my mom the name of an ankle and foot doctor in Austin, but he wasn't able to fit us in until the next morning. Because of that, I missed morning practice, and I had to take the first two periods off from school. I never thought I'd miss school, but even a pop quiz would be better than sitting in the cold waiting room, listening to the receptionist answer the phones "Dr. Michaels's office. How may I direct your call?"

By this time, I felt only a slight twinge in my

heel when I walked, and I was starting to think maybe I had exaggerated the paid the day before. The truth was that I was a huge drama queen—I knew that about myself. And this was one instance where maybe I had let my drama-loving ways get out of control. I'd landed and felt some pain, and I'd gotten scared. But it really wasn't a big deal.

Obviously, my mom was feeling the same way, because she was impatiently flipping through a magazine, cracking every page like a whip. There were articles about childhood obesity and human growth hormones in milk, two topics I knew my mom was interested in because she was always harping at me about health stuff, but she passed them by without a second glance.

"Does it hurt right now?" she asked me for the thousandth time, glancing down at my foot as though with x-ray vision she could see through my sneaker to some pulsing red dot of pain. We'd already had an x-ray of the area, actually, and an ultrasound, both of which Dr. Michaels was no doubt looking at that very moment.

"Not really," I said.

She drummed her French-tipped fingers on the armrest. Everything in Dr. Michaels's office was mauve or green, and there was a fake plant that kept tickling me if I leaned close to it.

"Dr. Chavez could've fit us in yesterday," she said. Dr. Chavez was the orthopedic doctor I'd seen once when I'd had some shoulder pain, which had turned out to be mostly the result of my sleeping on the shoulder badly. I'd started putting an extra pillow beneath me while I slept on my side, saw my massage therapist, Ivana, a couple of times, and everything was as good as new.

Dr. Chavez's office was also decorated a lot nicer, with these cool paintings on the walls, of random shapes and lines. I could stare at them for hours, trying to figure out what they were.

Just then, a nurse came out, holding a chart in her hands. "Aurelia Christina Flores?"

"Just Christina," I said, standing up and feeling suddenly nervous as my mom and I went back into the maze of offices. The nurse brought us to an exam room, where she proceeded to ask me questions about my foot and ankle, the pain I felt, and how long it had been going on.

"You're a gymnast?" she clarified, glancing at the sheet in front of her.

Any other time, I would proudly have said yes.

But now, I was worried less about impressing the nurse than that she might tell me I would have to stop training. I settled for nodding.

She had to look up from her clipboard to catch my answer. When she did, she smiled. "No doubt that's why Mo Li referred you to Dr. Michaels," she said. "He was a gymnast, too, back in college."

Wow. "Did he go to the Olympics?" I asked eagerly.

The nurse laughed and shook her head. "No, but he was very good." She turned to face my mother. "Dr. Michaels will be in shortly."

My mother made a sound like *harrumph*. She was probably wishing she'd found a doctor who had made it on an Olympic team, although even then she wouldn't rest unless he had a medal. Preferably gold.

Dr. Michaels didn't keep us waiting for too long. He came in with a big smile on his face, and even though I'd already steeled myself for someone mean and cruel and only out to crush my dreams, I couldn't help it. I immediately liked him.

He wasn't that old—I knew my mom would turn up her nose at that—and he was an inch shorter than she was in her heels. It was almost funny.

"Mrs. Flores?" He reached out his hand to shake hers, and she grudgingly took it. Then he turned to me. "Christina, hi. How are you doing today?"

"Okay," I said.

"So, you're feeling a little pain in your left heel and ankle area, is that right? Let's check it out."

I stretched my legs out on the crinkly paper of the exam table, and Dr. Michaels pressed several parts of my foot, ankle, calf, and shin. A couple of times, it hurt when he put pressure on a particular area, and I told him so.

Dr. Michaels also had me put my knees up and push my feet into the exam table, almost as though I was about to spring into a round-off. That hurt a little bit, and so I told him that, too.

It only took a few minutes until Dr. Michaels told me we were done. His tone was so easy and casual that I felt a weight immediately lift off my shoulders. Everything was going to be fine. There was nothing to worry about.

I was so caught up in this newfound relief that I didn't pay attention to what he was saying until my mother interrupted.

"Tendinosis?" she said. "What's that?"

The weight came crashing back down on me

like a balance beam falling from the sky. *Tendinosis?* That sounded serious.

Dr. Michaels's voice was still very even as he explained, "Achilles tendinosis is a degeneration of the Achilles tendon, where the scar tissue is less pliable and so causes pain. It's usually a chronic injury and can be caused by constant high-impact stress on the area. No doubt in Christina's case, it stems from the many hours she spends running, tumbling—anything that puts pressure on it."

He smiled at me when he said my name, but I looked away. I could feel the tears stinging in my eyes again like back in the gym, and I didn't want to cry now, either.

"That's the bad news," Dr. Michaels said. "The good news is that it could be much worse. From the ultrasound, I can tell that the Achilles hasn't ruptured, and at this point I see no need for surgery. But Christina is going to need to rest for a while."

My mother stood with her arms crossed over her chest, her fingernails digging into her skin. "How long is *a while*?"

"I would recommend at least six weeks," Dr. Michaels said. He delivered the news with the same pleasant tone he'd used throughout, but still he sounded like a judge laying down a prison sentence. "But of course, we'll check on her progress in follow-up visits."

He asked if we had any questions. My mom had several, although mostly she talked about how her husband was a cardiologist and one of the top doctors in his field and how old was Dr. Michaels, anyway? I tuned them both out.

Six weeks? The Invitational was in early February, so I would be better by then, but in the meantime, I couldn't train full routines. I couldn't run practice vaults, or tumble on the floor, or work on dismounts. How could I take six weeks off from all of that and still be ready for the Invitational?

The moment that played over and over in my head was the one when I landed on that mat in the gym and sank to my knees. Right now, I'd have given anything to take that moment back. I wished I had just gritted my teeth, stuck my dismount, and kept my pain to myself. Maybe then I'd have been working on my double Arabian, instead of sitting here in this doctor's office wondering if six weeks was long enough for my body to forget what a double Arabian was.

Five

When we got home, there was a Cadillac in the driveway that I'd never seen before, which meant my father must be back from his Ontario conference. He traveled so much that he didn't have his own car, so he rented cars wherever he was, even around Austin if he needed to check in on his cardiology practice or have the rare consultation with a patient. I didn't completely understand why my dad was such a big deal in the heart surgery world, although I knew he had come up with some kind of technique or treatment that was supposed to be awesomely groundbreaking.

Generally, I didn't care why he was a scientific genius. I cared that he was my dad and that I missed him when he wasn't around.

I jumped out of my mom's SUV and started running toward the house, but the sudden twinge in my heel reminded me that I shouldn't. It didn't stop me, though, from bursting through the door and heading right for my dad's office, where I knew I'd find him. "Daddy!"

He spun around in his desk chair, enveloping me in a huge bear hug. "Princess! I heard you were a little gimpy. Sorry I missed your appointment today—what'd the quack have to say?"

It was an old joke—my dad calling anyone in the medical field a quack (including himself)—but it still made me giggle. He could always make me laugh, even about something like this. "The doctor says Achilles tendinosis," I said. It was crazy how that word had felt so strange just a few hours ago and now sounded so familiar. "He wants me to rest, even though the biggest competition in my life is coming up. Maybe you could talk to him—tell him that you're a doctor and—"

He squeezed my hand. "Sorry, kiddo. The Achilles isn't exactly my specialty. If I tell my patients to rest, I expect them to rest, so you'd better listen to his advice."

It occurred to me that, after Ontario, he was supposed to have gone to some charity dinner for heart disease in New York City. "Are you here because of me?" I asked.

"Your mom called and told me about the injury," he said. "I took the first flight home."

I should have been upset that I'd made him miss an important event, but instead I felt a glow of happiness at the thought that he'd come home just for me. I hugged him again, tighter this time. "Thank you, Daddy."

My mother appeared and leaned against the doorway, watching us. I noticed for the first time that she looked a little tired. There were shadows beneath her eyes, and her shoulders slumped a bit, when normally she had close-to-perfect posture. She'd learned it taking ballet lessons when *she* was a young girl.

My dad stood up when he saw her and crossed over to kiss her on the cheek. He said something softly to her in Spanish, and she murmured something back before curling her arms around his neck and pulling him toward her for a hug. It had never really occurred to me that my mother might miss my dad, too. She saw him as infrequently as I did.

That night, we had dinner as a family, something we hadn't done for what felt like forever. My mom cooked my dad's favorite, empanadas, and even though I wasn't a fan, I kept my mouth shut and ate enough that my mom would think I liked them. After dinner, I usually would've gone down to the basement and done a few exercises at the barre that my parents had installed for me, or walked on the treadmill for twenty minutes, but of course now that wasn't a good idea. There was an awkward pause as we sat at the table, my mother silent, when usually she'd have been reminding me to keep up with my exercises. Now, those reminders were obsolete.

"Princess," my dad said. I perked up. "I brought you home something from Canada. Why don't you go into the study and look in my luggage? You can play with it right away."

My dad always got me the best gifts. My mother often gave me stuff like makeup or other beauty supplies or clothes. One Christmas, she'd given me this really nice straightening iron that wasn't supposed to damage your hair as much—something about the way it heated up slowly. I'd begged for it for months, but when I finally had it, I'd used it once and then stowed it underneath the sink and never touched it again.

I felt like an ungrateful jerk for even thinking that my mom's gifts weren't nice. It was just that my mom got me stuff I said I wanted, but ended up not really caring about as much as I had thought I would. I couldn't even count the number of unopened body lotions on my vanity or dresses hanging in my closet that still had tags on them.

Somehow, my dad managed to get me presents I hadn't even imagined, but after receiving them became my favorite things in the world.

So, as soon as I'd heard that there was a gift waiting for me in the study, I leapt up and practically ran to my dad's suitcase. I had to dig through his neatly folded shirts and throw aside a bag that ended up being filled with his toothbrush and toothpaste instead, but eventually I found it: a gymnastics computer game.

He'd said I could play it right away, so I popped it into my dad's work computer and eagerly waited for it to load up. Maybe this injury of mine wasn't such a bad thing after all. Where usually I'd have been on my tenth plié by now, I was getting to play games on the computer instead. Kind of a sweet deal.

When the welcome screen popped up, it told me to download the game to the desktop. I used my dad's computer all the time for school projects and to e-mail some of my family in Mexico, but I didn't want to do anything without asking him first. I headed back to the dining room to ask his permission to download the game, although I assumed it would probably be okay.

I was walking toward the dining room and could hear my parents' low voices. When I heard my name I stopped just outside the door. It was obvious that whatever they were discussing was important, and it was also clear that the conversation was getting a little heated. I could hear my mother's frustrated sigh, the one that meant she was sick of repeating herself. I'd heard that sigh a million times, usually on those long car rides home from the gym.

Then I heard my name and realized they were talking about *me*.

"It's not the end of the world," my dad was saying. "She has an overuse injury. She puts a lot of stress on her body; it's to be expected. She'll rest like the doctor is telling her to, it'll heal, and she'll be back to her old form in no time."

"You don't understand," my mom said. Her voice was quiet, but passionate. I could almost picture her eyes blazing, and the way she would impatiently sweep her hair away from her face, confronting him head-on. "It's not just about her Achilles. If Christina takes a break, she could lose focus. *I* could lose focus. Do you know how hard it is to keep her on track? Every day, driving her to practice, watching her, listening to her coaches, making sure she's following their directions, bringing her home, cooking her healthy meals, encouraging her to be disciplined. It's tiring. I'm *tired.*"

"Then maybe this will be good for both of you," my dad said. His voice was tense now, his words clipped.

"That's easy for you to say," my mom muttered. "*You're* never here."

There was silence for a moment. I decided to slip away. Instead of asking my dad about the computer game, or returning to the study to play it, I just went up to my room. The last thing I wanted to do was listen to my parents argue.

I resented my mother's implication that

without her, I would somehow completely fall apart. My gymnastics was like a full-time job for me. My mom didn't even have a job. If she was going to imply that I basically employed her, that I held her hostage with my gymnastics, then, fine. I would fire her. I could manage on my own.

I crawled into bed and waited, figuring that any minute now my mom would come in to say good night, or to see where I'd gone, since I wasn't in the study. As I lay there, I planned what I would say, and how I would act. Should I be cold and distant, letting her know that I'd heard what she had said? Or should I act normal and then talk to her about it later, at the right time?

My mind went around and around in circles; it was as exhausting as the laps Mo made us do around the floor. It wasn't long before I drifted off to sleep.

I missed the next day of school, too. My parents took me to the gym to talk to Mo. Apparently, Mo had said that it was fine for me to come in during early-morning practice and that we could discuss a plan for my recovery, but that wasn't good enough for my mother. She wanted to make sure we had all of Mo's attention, so we made an appointment for one o'clock.

It was really weird to be in the gym in the middle of the day. There were a couple of Tumbling Tots classes going on, and the kids were running around the blue floor mat like they owned it. During the Elite team training, the really little kids weren't around, because it was either early in the morning or late in the day. Now, they were doing somersaults and flying around the mats like they were on an obstacle course, and I wanted to scream at them, *It's not your floor! Get off it before you ruin it!*

But of course, that would have been totally psycho. There was no reason to yell at three-year-olds. Besides, it wasn't my floor, either.

It was also strange to be with my dad in the gym. I couldn't even remember the last time he'd set foot in there—maybe a Parents' Day event five years ago. As we headed toward Mo's office, he kept looking around and asking me questions like we were touring a museum. Stuff like *Is that where you do your balance beam routines?* and *How tall are those uneven bars, anyway?*

Mo got up to welcome us in to her office, and my mom and I sat down in the two chairs facing her desk, while my dad stood behind us. I'd been in Mo's office only a few weeks before, but it had been very different then. My mom and I had gone in to tell Mo about our plan not to take the stipend that had been offered as part of my making the National team. It had made sense to forgo the money in order to retain my amateur status, in case I wanted to compete in college. Back then, all my options had been open. Now, it felt like they were closing.

"We miss you today," Mo said once we'd settled in. She said it kindly, but it still felt like an admonishment. *Why weren't you at practice?*

I'd gotten the chance to sleep in until eight o'clock, almost three hours past my usual wake-up time, but it hadn't felt nearly as wonderful as I'd always imagined it would. Instead, I felt oddly sluggish.

My mother cut right to the chase. "The doctor said six weeks," she said, "but surely that can't be right? There's no tear. Even the ultrasound showed no tear."

Mo leaned forward, lacing her hands together on the desk. She seemed to be carefully considering her next words. "If you worry about Invitational, don't. She will compete. She will be fine."

Behind me, my dad squeezed my shoulder. "That's great news," he said.

But my mother had watched my practices long enough to know as well as I did that Mo's assurances weren't completely convincing. Even if I had had another month to train for the Invitational, the fact of the matter was that I was going to lose a ton of time on the sidelines. I was going to lose muscle. I was going to lose momentum.

"What about a cortisone shot?" my mom asked.

I glanced at my mom, but she was looking at Mo, completely serious.

Mo's lips tightened slightly; she shook her head. "Cortisone is for inflammation," she said. "What Christina have is not inflammation. In fact, it is more like her tendon wear down than flame up. We do not treat symptom; we treat cause."

I should've felt disappointment at her response. Although I'd never had a cortisone shot before, I'd heard of them—at the last Olympics alone, the rumor was that at least three of the American gymnasts had had cortisone shots in some part of their bodies to get them ready to compete. If that was what it would take to keep me practicing, I should have wanted one.

Still, I couldn't help feeling a little relieved that Mo knocked the idea down. Something about getting a big injection in that tender area at the back of my ankle . . . No, thank you.

"I only want what's best for Christina," my mom said stiffly. She glanced back at my dad; I couldn't tell whether she some wanted affirmation of the fact that she was looking out for me or agreement that a cortisone shot would do the trick.

"I know," Mo said. "We all do. That is why she need to rest, and get better. Then she come back even stronger gymnast than before."

Mo proceeded to outline my new training plan. When the team was on bars, I could work on my entire routine except for the dismount. When the team moved to beam, I could work on balance and dance elements, but no acrobatic series or leaps, which would have put stress on my Achilles tendon. On floor, I could also work on dance, but, of course, nothing heavier. While the other girls were lining up at the corners of the mat and tumbling back and forth, I would be on an exercise bike that they would move to the sidelines just for me, helping me keep up my stamina and develop my leg muscles while avoiding any hard impact.

Oh, joy. An exercise bike. Now, instead of training like an Elite gymnast, I could work out like any other random person in America.

The only upside was that I would no longer practice on vault. The prospect of taking a break from it was kind of appealing, but then again, this only meant I'd get further behind.

When Mo finished explaining my new training schedule, my mother reluctantly gave her approval. I knew she'd rather I had not been injured in the first place—as did I, obviously—but ultimately, she was looking for whatever would serve me and my career best, and she seemed to think that Mo's plan would get me to the Invitational.

"We have a workout space in our basement," my mother said, "with a ballet barre and parallette bars and a practice beam. So Christina will get plenty of time conditioning, believe me."

Mo took out a pair of reading glasses that I rarely saw her wear—even when she was reading something, she usually just squinted. She slid a piece of paper from underneath a weight shaped like the Texas Twisters logo—a gymnast leaping in a cyclonelike swirl—and examined it for a few moments before handing it to my mother.

"I talk with Dr. Michaels and draw up this plan," Mo said. "It has instruction for Christina at home and here at gym. One of things we do is let her *rest*. So there will be no extra work at home. I also think she should not do ballet. Too much stress on tendon."

My mother looked over the piece of paper Mo had handed her; beneath her makeup I could see a slight bloom of red on her cheeks. "Ballet isn't high impact," she said. "Christina rarely leaps around; you know that. She only does exercises at the barre to improve her flexibility and grace."

"Ballet involve flexing of tendon," Mo said. "Up, down, up, down. She is always stretching and bending and putting weight on it. That not good for her right now, so we take break. Yes?"

She looked from me to my mother to my father and back to me again. What could we say? When it came to my gymnastics, Mo was boss.

"Yes," I said.

As we left Mo's office, I glanced one more time at the toddlers on the floor. They didn't even know how to do a cartwheel, much less a double Arabian. Then again, they didn't know what Achilles tendinosis was, either. If they had had to stop gymnastics, they might have whined or cried, but they'd forget in a few weeks and move on to something else. They didn't know what it felt like to have a goal, much less how it felt to have that goal suddenly yanked out of reach.

Six

It had been kind of nice to take a couple of days off school, but of course I had to return eventually.

At lunch, Noelle and Britt were dying to know all the details.

"So, what does that mean, a 'chronic injury'?" Noelle asked.

Britt had been drinking from a juice box, but she let go of the straw so fast that she ended up dribbling apple juice down her chin. "*Chronic* means something that goes on for a while." Britt had been homeschooled by her supersmart grandmother and allowed to skip a grade in public school, so sometimes she liked to show off what she knew. Then she seemed to realize that she was talking about my injury here—my whole *life*—rather than reciting a word in a spelling bee. "Sorry, Christina," she said.

I shrugged, trying to pretend I didn't care. "I'll be back by the Invitational," I said. "That's all that counts."

"Back and better than ever," Noelle said, correcting me and grinning.

That was pretty much a repeat of what Mo had said, but it sounded like a lie no matter whose mouth it came from. How was I going to take six weeks off from hard-core training and get *better*? Like riding an exercise bike would somehow unlock my potential as a gymnast? Like it would make me magically able to double my vault difficulty, throw crazy tricks on the floor, fly over the bars as if I was made of air?

Yeah, right.

Not that it was bad to lie in this case. Noelle was trying to be a good friend and make me feel better, and of course Mo wasn't going to tell me that everything was now hopeless. But I could see that look in both Noelle's and Britt's eyes when they shared a quick glance—it said: *God, I hope that doesn't happen to me. Could it happen to me?* And I didn't blame them for that, either. It was natural to become protective and paranoid when you saw someone else get injured in gymnastics. You heard about someone else's stress fracture, and you started favoring one leg, worried that you were developing a stress fracture yourself. You heard about someone else's strained back, and you started worrying about that slight twinge you felt when you did a walkover.

"Why is it called the Achilles tendon, anyway?" Noelle asked. "Something to do with mythology, right?"

"Oooh, I know this one," Britt said, sitting straighter in her chair. Luckily, she'd finished with the juice, so we didn't have to worry about her spraying us with it in her excitement. She'd been known to knock over drinks with her expansive gestures. Once, she had even squirted milk out of her nose laughing.

"So, Achilles was this ancient Greek dude who fought with that guy from the Odyssey," Britt explained. "His mom dipped him the River Styx by holding him by the heel, making the rest of his body totally invincible, like the Incredible Hulk."

"Is the Hulk invincible?" I asked. "I thought he was just really big and strong."

In truth, I had no idea what I was talking about. I had seen a movie about the Hulk once, and it was so boring I'd fallen asleep in the middle of it. But interrupting Britt was fun, because she got all huffy.

"Anyway," she said pointedly, glaring at me, "Achilles had this one weak spot, which was his heel. So some other Greek guy shot him in it with an arrow, and Achilles died."

Britt's gaze flicked to mine on that last word, but she quickly looked away. Clearly, Noelle had had the same thought. She awkwardly moved her salad around with her fork. I mean, seriously, whose bright idea was it to tell a girl with an Achilles tendon injury that, *Oh yeah,* the dude who it was named for died because of it?

"There's this famous painting of Achilles that my grandmother showed me once," Britt finally went on. "My mom was mad, because I was only nine and the painting isn't shy about his you-know-what."

"What?" Noelle asked, before her face turned bright red. "Oh."

I couldn't help it—I started laughing. Britt joined in, and eventually so did Noelle, even though she was clearly still embarrassed. At least for those few moments, I forgot about my injury and the Invitational and gymnastics.

For Ms. Rine's class, we were supposed to have read a book that somehow pertained to our essay, then written a report on it. I had never gotten around to it.

Noelle had chosen a biography of Nadia Comaneci, naturally. I'd never actually read the book, but I knew her story. It was basically a fairy tale. Once upon a time, a girl gets discovered on the playground. She lives happily ever after with the first perfect ten score in Olympic history and tons of medals. The end.

Ms. Rine asked us to hand up our reports to the front of each row right before the final bell rang. I pretended to be searching through my backpack while everyone else turned theirs in. But of course, Noelle couldn't leave well enough alone. She twisted around in her seat, holding her hand out to me expectantly, even after I handed her the two reports from the guys who sat behind me.

"I don't have it," I muttered.

"Do you need help looking for it?" she said. "Did you check the front pocket?"

First of all, I never put homework in my

backpack's front pocket, which was big enough to hold a pencil case and that was it. Second, I wished Noelle would leave me alone. "I don't have it," I repeated, still trying to keep my voice low.

She drew her brows together. "Could you have left it at home?" she asked. "I bet Ms. Rine would understand. Or you could call your mom, and she could bring it."

I shook my head, hoping that Noelle would get the hint before Ms. Rine came over to our row. She continued to look confused, but at least she stopped pestering me. When Ms. Rine finally reached us, she took the three reports handed in without checking to see where the fourth one had gone. I breathed a sigh of relief.

The bell rang, and we packed up our stuff. I thought Noelle would drop the whole thing, but instead she waited until we were out in the hallway to harass me some more. What was she, the homework police?

"Didn't you do it?" she asked, her eyes wide. For Noelle, the idea of not doing homework was like not brushing her teeth, or not eating breakfast. These were all things I'd occasionally skipped without feeling too bad.

"I've been busy," I said. "You know, with the injury and everything . . ."

Noelle knew as well as I did that that was a cop-out. Once I'd gotten diagnosed with the tendinosis, stuff had gotten a little bit crazy, between the doctor appointment and missed practices and the extra tension at home. But if anything, I'd actually had *more* time to do schoolwork than before. I hadn't forgotten about this assignment, which we'd known about for weeks. I'd just pushed it back in my thoughts, telling myself that I would deal with it later.

After a few moments of silence, Noelle said, "If you give Ms. Rine a doctor's note, I bet she'll let you make it up."

"Maybe," I said.

She held out the biography. "Here, you can borrow this."

"I can't use the same book as you," I said. "Our essays are already similar enough. You said it yourself."

Noelle shrugged. "It's really good. I think you'd like it. If you decide to use it for your report, then I'm sure whatever you write about it will be different from what I wrote. And if you don't, at least it might give you an idea where to start."

I took the book, even though I had no intention of actually reading it. "Thanks."

All around us, people were chattering about their weekend plans or rushing to get to their next class. Noelle and I had different classes for the last period of the day. I was about to say good-bye when she cleared her throat.

"How does it feel?" she asked.

Naturally, I'd only ever imagined myself answering easy questions from gymnastics commentators, (like *How did you manage to win every competition this year?* or *What's the secret to your amazing toe point?*), but they were more likely to ask the hard ones. A gymnast would fall off the bars in this horrible, embarrassing mistake on her dismount, and the commentator would want to know how it *felt.* I loved Noelle, but I didn't particularly want to answer her question.

I didn't want to be rude, though, so I gave her the same answer I would have given if I were being interviewed on national television. I pasted a smile on my face and said, "It stinks, but I'll bounce back. I just can't wait to get out there on the floor again."

She looked a little doubtful, but then the

warning bell rang and we both had to hurry off to our classes. It was only later, when I was staring out the window of my second-floor classroom, that I started to wonder if she doubted that I was telling the truth about being okay with my injury, or if she doubted that I would ever come back.

At the next practice, I stretched with the other girls, although we split up once we were finished. Cheng took Britt, Noelle, and Jessie to the floor to work on their tumbling passes. Mo had moved an exercise bike out to the sidelines, but it still felt weird to be a spectator. I set the bike to an easy pace, just enough to keep my muscles warmed up without putting too much pressure on my heel, and watched the others as I pedaled.

Britt landed a double pike a little short, and I winced in sympathy. That kind of landing was exactly what Mo and Dr. Michaels worried could have made my injury worse, which was why I wasn't going to be allowed to do any tumbling for the next month. Noelle ran across the floor next and didn't quite make it all the way around on her triple twist. She tweaked her ankle slightly, her body facing forward as her feet angled, hitting the mat. Jessie drilled her landing on a double front tuck with a sound worthy of a cartoon.

I had done these skills over and over every day, and I was used to the aches and pains in my body when I went home, but it had never occurred to me how high-impact gymnastics really was. Now that I had been hurt, I couldn't help watching everyone else and noticing how easy it would have been for them to break a bone or tear a ligament. Worst of all, perhaps, were injuries like mine, which didn't happen because of one move but were the result of constant abuse. From my perch on the bike, I felt like I had x-ray vision and could see into everyone's ankles and Achilles tendons and shins and feet, and what I saw was kind of scary.

Mo told everyone to take a five-minute break; I was surprised to see Jessie cross over to me instead of joining Britt and Noelle over by the water fountain. "Hey," she said.

"Hey."

If she asked me what was up, I thought I'd scream. What did she *think* was up? All my dreams, maybe, up in smoke.

"I just wanted to tell you that I know how you feel," she said, her gaze serious as she looked at me.

Instantly I felt bad. I should've known that Jessie, of all people, would understand what a big deal it was to be on the sidelines when you should have been training for the most important competition of your life.

"When I was having the worst time with my eating disorder"—Jessie cleared her throat, and I realized that I'd never heard her say those two words out loud before—"one of the hardest parts was watching all of you guys practicing. I thought you would move on without me."

"We didn't," I assured her, even though that was all past now.

"I know," she said. She made a face. "But I wanted to let you know that you'll be back out there, too, before you know it."

I glanced out at the gym, the place I'd trained in for years and knew better than I knew my own house. It was strange to see it from this perspective, as more a spectator than a participant, like I was a tourist at the aquarium instead of one of the fish.

Jessie gave my shoulder a squeeze. "It's only a stupid tendon," she said. "It's physical, and when it comes to that kind of stuff, we're rock stars. We do things with our bodies that most people can't even dream of."

It's only physical. I smiled, because I appreciated what Jessie was trying to say, and even if we hadn't always been the closest friends, I knew she really cared. But right now, it felt like it was so much more than just a physical problem. It was mental and emotional and spiritual.

Jessie gave me one last wave before running out to the floor. Mo crossed over to me before joining the girls to help them work on their dances. "You can listen to music," she said, "and follow along with arms. Yes?"

I nodded, but I had no idea how I was going to do that. Dance with only my arms? It seemed silly. But if that was what Mo wanted me to do, then I wasn't going to argue. Especially with my mom seated right behind me in the parents' viewing area. *Do you know how hard it is to keep her on track?* I gritted my teeth and put in my earbuds.

The music for my floor routine had a saucy Latin swing to it, so at first it felt really awkward to wave my arms around with the usual flavor I liked to put into the movements, which made sense if you could see my whole body. The hand motions alone looked stupid.

By the time I was on my third rep, it was feeling

more natural. I closed my eyes as I danced through a slow section of my routine, which was meant to show off my grace, but also to give me a chance to breathe before my final pass. When I opened them, Noelle's oldest brother, Mihai, was standing next to me, clapping.

I scowled at him, removing my earbuds. "What?" I demanded.

"Can't I just admire your sweet moves?" he asked.

"No," I replied rudely.

He shrugged. "I heard about your ankle," he said. "Sorry."

Technically, it wasn't my ankle, but I didn't feel like correcting him. I'd had a bit of a crush on Mihai for a while, ever since Noelle and I had started hanging out. He was fifteen with dark brown eyes and dark hair that was a little too long, and he always seemed so *cool*. Under normal circumstances, I would've been happy that he was singling me out and paying attention to me, but these circumstances involved my looking like an idiot. So, yeah, I was less than thrilled.

Out of the corner of my eye, I could see my mother, who also looked less than thrilled that I was talking to a boy instead of working out. Mo wouldn't be pleased, either, but in that moment I didn't care. If my mom wanted to put herself in charge of my gymnastics, then, fine. Let her take charge of this.

"It's okay," I said to Mihai, shooting him a smile I hoped was dazzling. He looked stunned by it, but I couldn't tell if it was in a wow-this-girl-is-so-pretty kind of way, or more in a why-is-the-weird-girl-baring-her-teeth kind of way. "It gives me time to work on my biking skills, right?"

Apparently Mihai didn't think I was *too* strange, because he actually smiled back. "If you ever get tired of biking in place," he said, "you should come riding some time."

Oh my God, oh my God, oh my God. Were we flirting? Was Mihai flirting with *me*?

"Noelle and I bike home every day," he added, "but we sometimes go for a quick spin around on Sundays, too."

Of course. He was inviting me out with him *and* his little sister, a.k.a. my best friend. It wasn't flirting at all. This time, when I responded, my voice was noticeably cooler. "Sounds like fun."

He cocked his head, as though considering me. "You can't be waving your arms around like that, though. People will think you're signaling. Or that you're a nut."

"Thanks," I said, "I'll keep that in—"

"Christina!" For a moment, I didn't know if the voice was Mo's or my mom's, not because they sounded anything alike, but because I'd been expecting one of them to reprimand me at some point. This time it was my mother, who was standing up in the bleachers and glaring at me.

Mihai had the nerve to wave at her. "Hi, Mrs. Flores!" he called. Since Noelle and I had been friends for a while, our families knew each other, even though it wasn't like we were getting together for dinner parties or anything like that.

I could see that my mom was torn between being polite and sticking to her disapproving stare. Finally, she grudgingly lifted her hand. "Hello," she called back. I was sure she didn't remember his name. "Christina, don't you need to get back to work?"

The whole gym was watching us now, since we were having to yell back and forth to each other. Mo snapped her fingers at me, as if to say, *Get on with it*. As nice as it felt, in a way, to rebel against my mother, this type of attention was not really what I was looking for.

“Thanks for the tip,” I muttered, more in response to my mom’s question than anything else.

“No problem,” Mihai assured me.

I gave him a funny look until I realized he must’ve thought I was just responding to his advice about biking. I decided to leave it, giving him an apologetic glance as I put my earbuds back in and returned to my lame workout.

After the team was done with floor, they moved on to vault, yet another event that I couldn’t practice. Mo came over and told me I’d done enough on the bike for now, and that I could do press-to-handstand exercises on the floor if I wanted to work on my upper-body strength. I decided it was better than vault, but not by much.

From my position on the square of blue carpet, I could hear the girls talking as they waited for their turn at vault. Britt and Jessie were arguing again about song lyrics, Jessie saying that it was a love song and Britt that the guy actually sounded like a jerk if you really listened carefully.

Noelle walked back from her last vault, and Britt cornered her before she could take her place in line. She sang a couple of bars of the song, then demanded, “What do you think? He’s a jerk, right?”

Noelle shrugged. "I don't pay much attention to the radio," she said. "Sorry."

Jessie moved to the end of the runway, waiting for Cheng's signal before taking off.

Britt glanced at me, as if seeking another opinion for her poll about the song, but then her gaze slid away.

I'd actually heard the song she was talking about, and had my own take on it that was somewhere in between hers and Jessie's. I wanted to tell them that maybe it wasn't a question of whether he loved the girl or was a self-centered moron who treated her badly. Maybe it was about emotions that were more complicated than that.

But in spite of what Jessie had said earlier, it felt like I wasn't part of the team anymore. We could talk in lunch at school, but here I couldn't practice with them or participate in their chats. Jessie nodded at a quick comment from Mo and then joined the other girls in time to finish making her last point about the song. She was still strongly on one side, with Britt on the other and Noelle staying neutral. And there I was, right in the middle, but really nowhere at all.

Seven

That weekend, my parents asked me if I wanted to drive around the neighborhood and look at the Christmas lights. My neighborhood always went all out, with some houses having different themes each year, or neighbors pairing up to make one big display. It had even been featured on the news last year, although the public couldn't come see the lights, because I lived in a gated community. Sometimes I thought it was a little strange to make such a big deal out of decorating for only the neighbors.

Especially when some of those neighbors, like me, lived in the neighborhood but didn't even check out all the lights. Last year, Noelle had spent a night at my house during the holidays and we'd walked up my street to look at some of the displays, but I'd never really seen the whole shebang.

It also felt a little weird, because my parents almost never offered to take me anywhere when they were both around. My mom took me and my teammates to the mall or the carnival or stuff like that, but when my dad was in town, he was often too busy to commit to going out. My mom would cook her fanciest meals, and we might rent a movie that my dad would laugh at occasionally while mostly peering at his laptop, but that was it.

So, of course, I was excited to finally see the lights that everyone talked about, but also to get out of the house and do something with my parents. I even forgot to be mad at my mom for what she'd said about having to keep me on track, although thinking about those words made my blood boil again, so I pushed them back down.

My dad grabbed the keys to the SUV, and I jumped up from the couch, where I'd been cutting up some gymnastics pictures I had printed from the computer to use in a collage for Ms. Rine's essay. She hadn't said we needed to have a visual, but I figured it couldn't hurt, especially because I wanted to put off the actual writing as long as possible.

"Why don't we walk?" I asked. It was a nice night: chilly enough for my thick wool-lined jacket that I loved, but not so cold that I felt like I'd have to wrap my whole face in a scarf. Plus, it would make the experience last longer.

My mom looked uneasy, but my dad just patted my head, picking up a few strands of my hair and letting them drop back to my shoulders. "Your Achilles, Princess," he said, and I felt my mood deflate a little bit.

"I'm allowed to *walk*," I muttered. "I'm not an invalid." When we got outside, I didn't even ask to sit up front with them in the middle seat that folded down. Instead, I climbed into the backseat, and when my mom put Christmas music on the radio, I asked her to turn it up.

Our house had a relatively modest Christmas display, considering the way the rest of the neighborhood went crazy with decorations. The roof looked frosted with dainty white lights, which I always imagined would tinkle like harp strings if you ran your hand across them, even though I'd done that before and they totally didn't. The big tree in our front yard was also wrapped with white lights, and the bushes were covered in a fine netting of the same. *Elegant* was the word my mom always used in talking with the professional who came out to do the decorations every December. *Boring* is what I would have called it.

Take our neighbor, for instance. He had a jolly inflatable Santa on his roof, waving as though he was taking off after leaving the best presents ever. The lights covering the house were brightly colored, winking cheerfully as they ran in a bunch of different patterns.

My mom had referred to it as "tacky" while talking to one of her friends on the phone. But I thought it was fun.

My dad pointed to a house that had spelled out MERRY CHRISTMAS on its roof in lights, and my mom oohed and aahed over another house with the all-white scheme that she loved so much. The people in that house had put snowflakes in the trees and bushes out front, making it, in my opinion, just a little better than our house. I could tell my mom was thinking the same thing, because while she exclaimed over how pretty it was, I could see through the sliver between the front passenger seat and the window that her mouth had gotten tight.

"Next year," my dad said, "we'll do something different. Something huge. What do you think, Princess?"

I thought that if things went back to normal, he probably wouldn't be around next Christmas. But it was still nice that he was thinking about it, so I tried to sound positive. "Awesome," I said.

My mom turned around in her seat, smiling back at me. "In four years," she said, "we can buy lights in every color, and we can make the Olympic rings on our roof. What do you think? I wonder if there are any light-up gymnastics figurines." She glanced at my father. "Do those exist, honey? Or would we have to have one custom made? We could give them a picture of Christina and they could use it to create an outline of her leaping across our lawn."

"That sounds like a fire hazard," my dad said. "Look at that house with the blue angel. It's beautiful." His voice was totally pleasant, but I could tell by the way he immediately changed the subject that something was bothering him.

"Or an ice sculpture!" my mom said excitedly. It happened to be a quiet part of the song on the radio, so her voice sounded extra loud in the SUV.

"We couldn't have it up always, obviously, but it would make an amazing centerpiece for a party. Do you think by December people will still care about the Olympics? What am I saying? Of course they will."

My dad flicked on the signal light and made a turn into a cul-de-sac where there was a candy-cane lighting theme. Every house was striped red and white, with big fake candy canes lining the front walks and dangling from the trees. "Let's not get ahead of ourselves," he said.

I thought I hadn't heard him at first, since "Jingle Bell Rock" had started playing, kind of loudly. I leaned forward in my seat. "What?"

He glanced at me in the rearview mirror. "Nothing against you, Princess," he said. "You're an amazing athlete; you know that. I'm only saying, let's not get ahead of ourselves."

Did my own father not believe in me? As annoying as my mom's pushiness could be, at least she saw me on that Olympic podium. Sometimes, I thought she wanted it even more than I did. But it sounded like my dad was hedging his bets, like he was waiting until a few minutes before the race to put his money on a horse.

My mom seemed as stung as I was. "Miguel . . ."

My dad looked at her. "You know what the doctor said."

Now I was sitting so far forward in my seat the seat belt was cutting into my waist. "What do you mean?" I asked. "What did the doctor say?" *What weren't they telling me?*

"Nothing," my mom assured me. "Miguel," she said, more sharply than before.

"I deserve to know," I said. "If it's about me, I deserve to know."

We stopped in front of the coolest house in the whole neighborhood, one that was decorated to look like a castle, complete with a crown on a rounded part of the roof, and a huge Christmas tree made out of lights in the front yard. I didn't even care. I wanted to know what secret they'd been hiding from me this whole time.

My first thought was that I would never walk again, because that was the kind of thing I'd always seen in the movies, but of course that was stupid. I wasn't paralyzed. But maybe it was almost as bad. "Will I never do gymnastics again?"

My dad pulled the SUV away from the curb. Clearly, none of us was really paying attention to the display. "Nothing like that, Princess," he said. "Dr. Michaels only said that Achilles injuries are really tough, and that ones like yours, that result from chronic overuse, have a tendency to flare up."

"What does that *mean*?" I demanded. I hated that word, *chronic*, the one that Britt liked to use to show off her superior English skills. I'd even looked it up in the dictionary that day when I got home, and had had my worst fears confirmed. Apparently it meant "lasting a long time" or "happening frequently," both of which were not good things when it came to injuries.

My mother sighed. "It only means that you're lucky you didn't rupture your tendon," she said, "but that even if it heals now, it doesn't mean you might not injure it again. It's possible you could have problems with that Achilles for the rest of your career."

There was that word again. *Lucky.*

"Or for the rest of your life," my dad added. He said it in a totally detached voice, like he was talking to a patient instead of his own daughter. I hated when he got like that.

How was any of this lucky?

He started to turn down another street, but I

leaned forward and grabbed the back of his seat. "Take me home," I said.

"What?" my dad asked.

The radio was blaring "Santa Claus Is Coming to Town" and I had to shout to be heard over it. "I want to go home!"

So my dad went right instead of left, back toward our house. And even though I'd insisted on this, it didn't really solve my problem. I didn't want to be trapped in this car with my parents anymore, but I didn't really want to go back into the same house as them, either. I wished there was a way I could escape to someplace else, a place where the body really could be invincible, and one stupid arrow to your heel couldn't result in your downfall.

Noelle's birthday was on Christmas Day, but she had her party a little before, the Sunday after school let out for the break. I mean, who's going to come out *on* Christmas?

The first few years I was friends with Noelle, I'd always assumed that that was the main reason why she never had a birthday party—because her birthday was too close to the holidays, and people were spending time with their families or going out of town. It was only in this last year that I had realized that Noelle's family didn't have as much money as mine or Jessie's or even Britt's. Lots of stuff like parties and new clothes for school and tickets to gymnastics events were luxuries that they couldn't afford.

I thought again about Ivana, who I'd just gotten to see earlier that week for a massage, and about the new custom leotards I knew were wrapped up under our tree at home. Each one cost a couple of hundred dollars, easily.

It made me kind of feel bad about the gift I'd gotten Noelle. If it had been anyone else, I would've gotten a really expensive makeup kit for her that included everything for doing a smoky eye, because I'd gotten one and it was awesome. Right now, my mom only let me use it for dress-up; I couldn't wait until I was in high school, able to wear that kind of makeup for real.

But it wasn't anybody else. It was Noelle, and she didn't really care about makeup, so that choice was out. And then I thought about getting her a custom leo, but I knew she would feel weird about it and probably wouldn't wear it much to practice because she'd be self-conscious about it.

So I ended up making her a collage. It was actually the same one I'd started for Ms. Rine's essay, but I knew that Noelle would appreciate it more than anyone else in the world. Because I'd found all the gymnastics pictures on the computer, I was able to include a lot of her absolute favorite gymnasts, ones from a while ago that most of us hadn't even heard of, like Daniela Silivaş, Olesya Dudnik, and Roza Galieva. I found a small picture of Noelle's mom when she was a gymnast back in Romania that was a little pixelated, but I tucked it into the collage because I knew Noelle would like it. Then, smack in the middle, I put a picture of Noelle herself, from when she'd been featured in the newspaper after that USA vs. the World event.

I also decided to write a poem to go along with the collage, arranging the letters in Noelle's name in a line going down the page to start me off. ***N**ational beam champion, what else could you want? **O**lympic gold, that's what you'll flaunt!*

When I'd finished, I'd felt really proud of myself, but now I was starting to have my doubts about the gift. The only money I had spent on for the collage had been for some special decoupage paste and another color printer cartridge. Wouldn't Noelle expect something expensive from me, something she couldn't buy herself?

I was still having my doubts when I arrived at Noelle's party, but then she was coming over to me and it was too late for me to get anything else even if I'd wanted to. I placed my gift on a table in her family's store that was normally reserved for a display of Eastern European coffees, but was now stacked with a few gifts.

"Christina!" Noelle smiled when she reached me.

"Hey," I said. "Happy birthday!"

Jessie was already there; she waved at me. Britt arrived a little later and spent the first thirty minutes of the party reciting every song lyric she could think of about getting the party started, how parties didn't start until she walked in, how she was coming up, so you'd better get the party started.

Finally, Noelle covered her ears. "It's my party," she said, "and I'll cry if I want to. Which I will, if you don't stop!"

Britt had brought Twister for us to play, although she asked us, like, eight times if we were sure we wanted to play it. But it ended up being a ton of fun—there's something about getting four gymnasts together and making them bend and stretch and flex. It was like a hilarious version of what we did every day. At one point, Jess and I had our arms wrapped around each other like we were a single pretzel, and then Jessie sneezed, causing both of us to fall on our butts.

Noelle won, although Britt had a melodramatic collapse toward the end of the game that made me wonder if she'd thrown it somehow, letting the birthday girl win.

"I know what you did," Noelle said, laughing. "You'd better bring your A game to the Invitational, though!"

"Oh, don't worry about *that*," Britt said. "If you think you have half a chance of winning, you are totally mistaken."

Later, we had cake that Noelle's mom had baked herself, and then Noelle opened her presents. Jessie gave her a subscription to *Flip for Gymnastics*, which was a great idea—I wished I'd thought of it. Britt gave her a T-shirt that said BOYS ARE DOGS, which I knew she'd gotten to make Noelle blush. Even though Noelle was getting close with this guy David from school, she adamantly swore she would never have a boyfriend until she'd won an Olympic medal.

Of course, for Noelle, that was pretty much guaranteed to happen. If I had made that same vow, I'd probably die surrounded by my cats.

I didn't even have time to figure out where *that* negative thought had come from when Noelle reached for my gift.

"It's not much. . . ." I said as she carefully slid her fingers underneath the tape on the wrapping paper.

The red polka-dot paper fell away, and Noelle gasped. Like, actually gasped. I hadn't realized how important it was to me that she respond well to my gift until I heard that.

"You like it?" I asked, although I could tell that she did. She was looking at each picture in turn, brushing over the one of her mom with her fingers. When she looked up, there were tears in her eyes.

"I *love* it, Christina," she said. "The poem is awesome. And I had no idea you were such an artist!"

"I'm not," I assured her. "I mean, I play around with it sometimes, just for fun, but it's not like I know what I'm doing. It's not much more than a second grader would do with scissors and glue."

"No, she's right," Britt said, looking over Noelle's shoulder. "This is *really* good. How much would it cost for me to commission one?"

"What?" I asked, not because I didn't hear her, but because I was totally floored by the question.

"My grandmother says art is an investment," Britt said. "So I want to know how I can get my hands on one of these for myself."

I didn't know how to respond, so I made a couple of flustered noises; then Mihai came to check out the present, too.

"Wow," he said, pointing at the picture in the center. "There's you! And hey . . . that's Mom! Mom, you've gotta come over here and see this."

The next ten minutes became a whirlwind of questions about how I'd made it, how I'd found the pictures, how long I'd been doing artwork, how I came up with the poem. I kept trying to explain that it wasn't that hard, that simple internet searches had turned up a lot of really cool pictures, and that art and poetry weren't really something I *did* so much as goofed around with, to relieve some stress once in a while. I was really glad that Noelle liked her gift, but all the attention was overwhelming.

When I was finally able to get away, I took refuge near the storage room door, a little apart from the rest of the party. For some reason, I was feeling a bit claustrophobic, like I needed to sit down and breathe. I didn't know why. It was just a party, and just a stupid present.

"You okay?"

Mihai had come over and was looking at me with those warm brown eyes. They were a lot like Noelle's, but whereas she always seemed in the middle of some serious thinking, he always had a glint in his eyes as though he were smiling even when he wasn't.

"I'm fine," I said. "I'm tired, that's all." I didn't want him to think I was some freak who couldn't even attend a party without getting weird. And usually, I wasn't. I loved parties. But that day, I felt weak and a little fragile. It was odd.

"Your present was seriously awesome," he said. "Thanks for blowing my *Stick It* DVD right out of the water."

"That's one of her favorite movies," I said quickly, "and I know—"

Mihai laughed. "Relax, I'm kidding. It's great to see Noelle happy, and I don't care if it's because of my present or your present or because aliens are taking over the moon. I just wanted to tell you that you did an amazing job."

He inclined his head toward the rest of the crowd. "Not that you needed to hear it from me," he said. "You might have to quit gymnastics and open an art studio, or start making greeting cards or something."

Quit gymnastics. Even though I knew Mihai was joking, something about those words caused my heart to do this funny flip. It was like having butterflies in my stomach, only instead they were in my chest. What was that feeling? Dread? Terror? Relief?

I gave an awkward laugh, just to let Mihai know that I still had a pulse. My mind was racing. Quitting gymnastics was the last thing I wanted to do. But still, those two words were ones I'd never allowed myself to put together in my head, and now that they were there, it was like I couldn't get them out. It was the opposite of that double Arabian I couldn't seem to visualize, where over and over I saw the words streaming like one of those banners attached to the tail of an airplane: *Quit gymnastics, quit gymnastics, quit gymnastics.*

Christmas in my house was always a huge deal, with a ten-foot-tall tree with a huge stack of presents beneath it wrapped in every different kind of wrapping paper my mother could find. Not all of the gifts were for me—some were for my cousins back in Mexico. Once, I'd asked my mom why she wouldn't ship them *before* the holiday, so that they could open them on Christmas morning. She'd simply said that then we wouldn't have them to look pretty under our tree, and that she was sure that my cousins appreciated having a second Christmas when the real one was over.

It struck me as odd to have half the presents under the tree be for people who weren't even there to open them, but I had to hand it to my mother: our tree did look like a department-store display, decorated in blue and silver, with gifts in packages of every color imaginable heaped up underneath it.

I opened my presents. They were pretty much the same things she always bought for me—perfumed bath lotions, gymnastics gear, and lots of clothes. When I opened my eighteenth new cardigan (maybe I was exaggerating, but not by much), I made a face.

Of course, my mother noticed this immediately. "What?" she said. "Do you not like purple anymore? I thought it was your favorite color."

It had been my favorite color two years ago, but

that wasn't the problem. The sweater was beautiful, as all the clothes my mother bought me were. It was made of really soft material, with a line of dainty, iridescent buttons running up the front.

"I was hoping for a watercolor set," I said.

The moment the words were out, I was horrified at myself. Here I was, sitting on the hardwood floor of our living room surrounded by boxes and bags filled with all kinds of stuff just for *me*, and I was being a total brat. I *knew* I was, even as I belligerently set my chin and looked my mother in the eye.

Her face was frozen, as though she couldn't believe what she was hearing. "Excuse me?"

"How many sweaters can I wear?" I asked. "I wanted something I could actually *use*, like a set of watercolors. In case you hadn't noticed, I like art. Why do you think I'm always sketching little things and cutting pictures out of magazines?"

My mother seemed too stunned to be mad. It was the calm before the storm. I knew that she would blow up eventually, but for right now, everything was very quiet. "I didn't know you liked art," she said.

"Yeah, like you didn't know that *red* is my favorite color now," I said. "Red!"

At that moment, my dad returned from the kitchen, where he'd been fixing himself an apple-spice tea. He glanced down at the sweater in my hands, and back up at my face. "That's purple, honey. You might need your eyes checked."

"She knows it's purple," my mom said. Her lips were so tight she didn't even flash a glimpse of her white teeth. Now she was getting mad. "Your daughter is upset because it's not red, or because it's not an art set, which she apparently wanted despite the fact that she never said a word about wanting one."

"That's why it's called a *surprise,*" I sneered. "If you get everything you ask for, it's boring."

If it weren't for the fact that my dad was super-healthy for his age—it kind of went with his job, since it would have been embarrassing if one of the world's leading heart doctors had clogged arteries—I thought he might have been about to have a heart attack. He set his tea down on the coffee table, probably to prevent himself from throwing it at me.

"Young lady," he said—he almost never called me that—"you do *not* talk to your mother like that, do you hear me?"

I stared at him until he repeated his question. This time, he practically yelled it.

"Yes, I hear you," I snapped. "The whole neighborhood hears you."

"What is wrong with you?" he asked. Only it didn't sound like he was truly concerned about my well-being. More like he'd discovered a demon sitting in his own living room, and was trying to figure out how it got there.

What was wrong with *me*? Gee, I don't know. I hadn't really been able to do gymnastics for a couple of weeks, and I imagined I could feel my muscles atrophying underneath my skin, like those astronauts do who go into space for a year and then can't even walk right when they come back. One minute, I'm dying to return to the sport I've been doing my entire life, and the next minute, I'm wondering why I care so much. In five years, will I have that Olympic gold medal? And if not, will all of this pain and struggle feel totally pointless?

Over on the couch, my mom had started to cry. It was quiet at first, but then she let out a sniffling sob that, in my uncharitable mood, I chalked up to her being a total drama queen for my dad's benefit. She was turning him against me.

"Why don't you go to your room," my dad said,

"and think about the true meaning of Christmas? Because I don't think you get it."

"I don't think *you* get it," I muttered.

My dad always did make an effort to come home for Christmas, but he would be locked back up in his study by the afternoon, trying to squeeze in a bit of work before dinner. Today, I knew, would be no different. By sending me to my room, he was getting a chance to start on his work a little earlier. He was probably relieved.

I knew he had heard what I'd said, because he drew his brows together and gave me a look like I'd be really sorry if I didn't get my butt up the stairs in five seconds. So I stood up and stomped out of the room, still holding the stupid sweater in my hands.

Before I was even at the staircase, I heard the low hum of my parents' voices behind me, and I knew that they were talking about me. Again. This time, I wasn't even tempted to turn around and eavesdrop. Let them say whatever.

When I got to my room, I threw myself on the bed. They were acting like I was the worst person in the world, when really all I had done was actually say what *I* wanted for once. It was always about the ballet lessons my mom thought I should take, or the floor music she thought the judges would like, or the lipstick she thought matched my skin tone. It was never about me. For once, I just wanted it to be about me.

But then I looked down at the sweater. It was more lilac than purple, and the buttons were almost like opals. Years of shopping with my mom had taught me to check the labels, and I wasn't surprised when I read that the cardigan was eighty percent cashmere. It was really soft and pretty.

I buried my head in it, and cried until eventually I fell asleep.

Eight

Noelle called the day after Christmas to see how mine had been. I didn't want to tell her about how I'd been a total brat and spoiled the entire day—it wasn't exactly my proudest moment. And yet she must've been able to hear in my voice that it hadn't been a very good couple of days, because later that afternoon, she showed up on my doorstep.

When I opened the door wider, I saw that Britt and Jessie were there, too.

"What is this?" I asked.

"It feels so weird to have the day off from practice," Britt said. "So Noelle called us up, and we figured we might as well head over here."

Wow. It was a superthoughtful idea, and exactly what I needed to bring me out of the funk I'd been in, but I didn't think I deserved it. Plus, even if I wanted to have them over, I doubted my mom would let me. I had assumed I was grounded, though I'd never been grounded in my life. Grounding me was something that I'm sure my mom didn't need any training to know how to do. It was, like, in the parents' manual that they get when you're born, and I'm sure if ever there was an offense worthy of grounding, ruining Christmas would be it.

My mom had come to stand behind me to see who was at the door, and I turned around. "Please?" I said. "They came all this way to see me."

Jessie's mom waved from behind the girls. "Hi, Mrs. Flores," she said. "Sorry to drop in on you like this, but the girls thought it would be a good idea to have an impromptu team meeting, since there's no practice today."

Those were the magic words. If it had something to do with gymnastics, my mother couldn't *not* say yes. It was programmed into her even deeper than that parents' manual stuff.

"Come on in," she said.

Jessie's mom said she would come back to get them in a few hours. The four of us went up to my room. Once I'd closed my door, I saw Britt look at Noelle, and Noelle nod at her.

"Uh . . ." I said, "what's going on?"

"We're here to stage an intervention," Noelle announced.

I'd never actually seen the TV show where people intervened with their family members or friends who had drug problems or were addicted to video games. My mom wouldn't let me watch it. But I'd heard enough about it that I knew the basic gist, and I was completely lost as to how I qualified for an intervention. "I'm sorry," I said. "What?"

Britt glanced around my room and frowned. "Usually the people all sit in a circle in chairs," she said. "Can we bring chairs from the kitchen up here?"

"We're not going to drag the kitchen chairs up here," I said, annoyed. "Tell me exactly what you guys are talking about."

Noelle seemed less sure of herself now, but she raised her chin and faced me. "You seemed down on the phone," she said, "and—"

Even though I knew it was really nice of them

to consider coming over to cheer me up, the overblown drama of it all made me roll my eyes. "I'm not going to sit in the dark and listen to sad songs or anything," I said. "Yesterday wasn't as much fun as I thought it would be. That's it."

And it had been all my fault. But I didn't feel like going into that part, so I left it out. They probably thought I was some spoiled brat who was pouting because she hadn't gotten what she wanted for Christmas, but if they had known the truth—that I'd actually pitched a fit and made my mother cry—even my own friends would probably have looked at me like I was psycho.

"It's not just yesterday," Noelle said. "Ever since you got hurt, it's been like you don't think you're part of the team anymore."

I plopped down on my bed. "Well, it's hard when I don't even get to practice with you guys half the time. And you're all getting ready for the Invitational, learning bigger and better skills, while I'm . . . stuck. I mean, come on. I ride a stationary bike every day. It's like a metaphor for my whole life."

Noelle brightened. I could tell she was happy to hear me use one of Ms. Rine's vocabulary words.

Before she could ask me about my essay—which I still hadn't written, despite its being due right after the break—I changed the subject.

"So, how, exactly, were you guys going to *intervene*, anyway?" I asked, waggling my eyebrows. "Tell me that you wouldn't love me anymore unless I shouted 'Texas Twisters' out my window at the top of my lungs? Did you write letters saying how much my lack of team spirit has hurt you?"

Jessie giggled, grabbing a pillow from my bed and throwing it at me, but Noelle had that same look in her eyes that she got when she was trying to make her little brothers behave. "Poke fun all you want," she said, "but we were worried about you."

"We only wanted you to know that we're here for you," Jessie said. "Like when I had to get treatment for my eating disorder, I was really scared. But I knew that you guys would always support me."

Gymnastics was a demanding sport, and it was true that each one of us had struggled in the past year. It had been in this very room, actually, that Britt had first revealed Jessie's big secret. And Jessie was right. It had been a challenge for us as a team, but we had gotten through it. It had been hard at first to accept Britt into our group when she moved to Texas, but now she was one of us. There had been a scary time when we'd thought maybe Noelle wouldn't have the money to compete at Nationals, but we'd held a special fund-raising car wash and done everything we could to raise the money for her to do it.

"You're part of this team, Christina," Noelle said, "whether you're on the sidelines or on the floor. You're a Texas Twister."

They were all being so honest and awesome, I felt like I had to return the favor. I had to tell them what was really on my mind. "I'm just scared," I said. "The doctor said that this injury could be something that flares up for the rest of my career, so who knows if it's going to affect my chances of going to the Olympics someday?"

I expected a moment of stunned silence, or maybe a quick assurance that I would heal perfectly and be good as new. But instead, Britt shrugged. "So what?"

"So what?" I repeated. "We're talking about my entire *career*."

"Yeah, but all kinds of things can affect your chances of going to the Olympics," Britt said. "It's four years until then. A ton of stuff can happen. I could get offered an amazing opportunity with the circus and blow this Popsicle stand. Jessie could hurt her knee in a freak Rollerblading accident and never compete again. Noelle could get in so much trouble with that *Lord of the Dance* guy for using his music that they won't allow her anywhere near the Olympics."

"It's *Riverdance*," Noelle said correcting her, but Britt barreled on.

"The point is, none of us knows what our future holds. But I can tell you what today is all about."

Britt had an impish grin on her face that I didn't trust. It was the same look she got when she was planning on playing some kind of prank. "What's that?" I asked warily.

"You screaming out the window that you're a Texas Twister," Britt said.

"What?" I did a pretty good imitation of that snort she always does. "No, I don't think so."

"I have to admit, I kind of liked that suggestion when you made it earlier," Jessie said.

"There's no way," I said, but I was laughing now.

"Come on." Noelle tugged at my arm, pulling me off the bed. "Do it, and we'll consider this intervention over. Promise. No letters about how much you're hurting us or anything."

"That's because I'm *not* hurting you," I said. "But you're hurting me. God, take my arm out of its socket, why don't you?"

But I let her drag me over to the window, where she unlocked and opened it. Immediately, the cold air hit me in the face. I shivered. I was only wearing a tank top, after all.

"It's freezing!" I said. "Close the window."

"Scream it first!" Jessie said.

"This is a gated community," I said in my haughtiest voice. "Do you have any idea what my neighbors would do if they—"

"Scream it, scream it!" Britt chanted.

Noelle was still standing next to me, with Britt on my other side. I reached behind me to pull Jessie nearer to us. "We'll all do it together," I said. "On the count of three . . ."

"One . . ." Noelle glanced at me and grinned.

"Two . . ." Britt rubbed her hands together and said something under her breath about how it *was* cold.

"Three!"

It may sound dumb, but shouting, "Texas Twisters!" from my window actually did help me feel like I was part of the team again. When we returned to practice the next day and I had to get back on the stationary bike, dancing with only my arms while the other girls practiced their routines on floor, I didn't even mind. Not that long ago, I'd actually considered quitting gymnastics, but now I knew that that wasn't at all what I wanted to do. Even if it meant that I had to spend the next few weeks on the sidelines, the other girls were right—I was still a Texas Twister at heart.

At least this time, I noticed Mihai enter the gym, so I wasn't surprised when he came up behind me. Lately, he'd been arriving at the end of practice, so that Noelle and he could ride their bikes home together.

Sometimes, like this day, he came a little early, and he would talk to me.

"The great arm dancer, hard at work," Mihai said. "You're, like, the opposite of those *Riverdance* people, huh?"

I snorted, although I did stop making my silly-looking arm movements and went back to just holding the bike handles. You know, not because I was self-conscious or anything, just because I needed a break. "What are you talking about?"

"Those dancers," Mihai said, as though that was helpful. "They always do this crazy stuff with their legs, but their arms stay straight at their sides. You're the opposite."

"Sounds like *someone* knows an awful lot about *Riverdance*," I said.

Apparently, that struck a nerve, because Mihai flushed. "You know Noelle's using the music," he muttered. "So of course she's always watching this one video of it over and over. It's practically shoved down my throat, that's all."

"Suuuure," I said. But I gave Mihai a sidelong smile to let him know I was only kidding.

He was silent for a moment. Finally I stopped pedaling long enough to look directly at him. I hoped I hadn't really offended him. I didn't honestly see what the big deal was about watching a dance video, but I could see how a boy might be sensitive about that kind of stuff.

I was about to apologize when he cleared his throat.

"So," he said, "did you give any more thought to the biking thing? If this arm-waving, stationary-bike gimmick is getting boring, you should give the real thing a try."

"I don't even know if I own a bike," I said truthfully. There might have been one in my garage, but biking had never been a hobby of mine, so my parents could've given my bike away or sold it when they noticed that I didn't use it.

He rubbed the back of his neck with his hand, like he had a mosquito bite or something else that was itching. "You might be able to use Noelle's," he said. "You guys are about the same height, right?"

Noelle was several inches shorter than me, but I didn't know if that mattered. Now it was my turn to flush, although I hoped Mihai would just blame it on all the exercising I'd been doing. I started pedaling again, faster than before. Maybe that would seem to provide a logical reason for why I was suddenly out of breath.

"Cool," I said, but it came out sounding like a wheeze. "I mean, awesome."

I'd assumed when Mihai first invited me to come over to his house and go biking with him that he meant with both him and Noelle. And while I was now kind of excited at the idea that it might wind up being Mihai and me alone, it also made me a little nervous. What would Noelle think about that?

Apparently, Mihai was having similar doubts,

because he backpedaled so quickly that he could've matched me for speed. "It's not a big deal if it doesn't work out," he said. "I'm pretty busy myself. When I'm not at school, I'm working at the store all the time now."

I flicked a glance toward the front desk, where my mother had been helping to answer the phones and process paperwork all afternoon. She was deep in some conversation with the lady who covered the pro shop, so I figured it was okay for me to talk to Mihai a little bit longer.

"Are you getting a lot of customers or something?"

It would be good if they had been. Noelle had said that there wasn't exactly a huge market for Romanian baked goods and groceries, but the two times I'd been in the store, I'd thought it was really nice. And last Easter, Noelle had brought in this sweet bread her mom had made called cozonac, which was totally amazing.

"Yeah," Mihai said, "but mostly I'm trying to save some money for college."

"College? That's not for a while."

Mihai gestured to the gym. "Yeah, but not all of us can rely on this to get us there. My grades aren't great. I only started turning them around this year, so I'm going to need all the help I can get."

"Gymnastics isn't going to get me into college," I said. I didn't want to admit that my grades might have been slipping, too. Ms. Rine had allowed me that extension on the book report, and I was supposed to turn it in with my final essay, but so far I hadn't done anything on either project.

Mihai looked at me like I was crazy. "Then why didn't you take the stipend?" he asked.

Normally, I thought of Mihai as being totally separate from the world of gymnastics. Even now, as he sat on the bench next to me chatting while I worked out, I didn't really associate him with gymnastics. So to hear him refer to something from my gymnastics life felt strange, like seeing a teacher outside of class. "What?"

"That stipend that they give you as part of the National team," Mihai said. "It was a topic at our house for a month, it felt like. My mother was worried that Noelle would jeopardize her chance at a college scholarship by taking the money; my dad said that she was smart and wouldn't need a gymnastics scholarship; my mom said but then she couldn't compete on the college team, either; my dad said why would she need to compete on the college team if she had the Olympics . . ."

He raised his eyebrows at my blank stare. "Come on," he said, "surely you had these kinds of conversations in your house."

Not really. After that woman from USAG came to talk to all of us about whether or not we were going to accept the money, my parents had decided that we wouldn't. We didn't need it that much to pay for my training, after all, and we figured we would keep my options open. But now that I thought about it, I'd never actually been part of that conversation. I assumed that my mother and father had talked about it, but never had they actually sat down with me and said, *Hey, Christina, what do* you *think?*

"Your parents talked to you, or to Noelle?" I asked. It was suddenly important for me to know.

"Oh, my God," he said, laughing a little. "It felt like they talked to *everyone*. I heard Tata on the phone discussing it with our uncle in Romania. But it was Noelle's idea to take the money. She said that they'd already sacrificed so much it seemed stupid not to."

I looked over at my mother, who had finished talking to the pro shop woman and was heading back toward the parents' viewing area. I wondered what she thought about my going to college, if she wanted me to be part of a team, like Noelle's mom wanted her to. I put my head down, pedaling for dear life.

Mihai must've gotten the not-so-subtle hint that this conversation was over, because he stood up. "Noelle has your number, right?" he asked. "I can get it from her. . . ."

I knew from the way he trailed off that my mother must have been right next to us, but I pretended I was so focused on my workout that I didn't notice her. It wasn't until Mihai said, "Hi, Mrs. Flores," that I even glanced up.

"Hello, Mihai," my mom said. At least she remembered his name this time, although it was the least friendly hello I'd ever heard in my life.

Mihai glanced between the two of us. "Well . . ." he said. "Uh, I think I'm going to wait for Noelle outside. I'll see you later, Christina."

As he headed out the front doors, my mother followed him with her gaze as though he were a lizard she wanted to make sure was completely out of the house before she relaxed. "What were you two talking about?" she asked.

Ever since Christmas, my mom and I hadn't been on the best of terms. We weren't fighting or anything—actually, quite the opposite. My dad had had to leave the day before, and my mother and I had barely spoken to each other the whole time he'd been there. After spending years wishing she would get off my back a little bit, now that she had, it felt kind of weird.

"College," I said. It was the truth, after all.

Her eyes registered surprise for a moment, and I didn't know if it was because I had said I was thinking about college or if it was because she hadn't thought Mihai was the type to care. She opened her mouth to speak. I tried to think about how I would answer any questions she might ask. Would I tell her that I was wondering why they hadn't talked to me about the stipend money? Would I ask her if she believed a college education was as important as the Olympics?

But my mom changed the subject. "While you were doing that," she said, her disdainful tone on the last word letting me know what she thought of my conversation with Mihai, "I talked to Mo about letting you work on a new release skill to add to your bar routine."

I was genuinely confused. "But you were talking to Mrs. Ivanek at the pro shop. . . ."

"Before," my mother snapped. "I meant I talked to Mo before. She and Cheng are going to think about what kind of skill you could do, and you might even be able to start working on it in bars practice tomorrow."

"Wow," I said. "Mom, thank you so much—"

I really meant it, too. Sometimes I got frustrated with my mother's meddling and controlling, but it was a great idea to up the difficulty in my bar routine, since it was the only one that I could really practice as long as I was laid up with this injury.

But my mother was already walking away, without even a *you're welcome.*

That Sunday, I told my mom I wanted to hang out with Noelle, so she took me by the store. I felt kind of guilty for lying to my mom—of course it was always nice to see Noelle, the truth was that I was going there mostly hoping to see Mihai.

But if I felt bad for misleading my mom a little bit, I felt really bad when I saw the smile that lit up Noelle's face as she let me in. "Hey," she said. "What's up?"

For a long time, Noelle hadn't even liked for me to see inside her apartment, and she definitely hadn't been happy to have me drop by unexpectedly. It made me feel guilty to realize how much she'd changed, and I hadn't really been close enough with her to see it.

I didn't want to be superobvious and ask about Mihai, and I really didn't want Noelle to think I was only there for her brother, who for all I knew thought I was some dumb kid. "Not much," I said. "Just felt like getting out of the house."

We pulled up stools to the front counter of the store. It was closed at the moment, so it was dim and quiet, although I could hear from the loud stomping above us that things weren't so calm upstairs. With four brothers, Noelle must always have felt like she was in the middle of chaos in that apartment.

I didn't know if Noelle caught my quick glance toward the door, or if she had just been watching me and Mihai talking at the gym, but the first thing she said was "Looking for Mihai?"

Busted. "Not really," I said, blushing.

She rolled her eyes—something that I did a zillion times a day but which Noelle reserved for those times when she was really exasperated about something. “You can say it,” she said. “I know you like him. You’ve always said you thought he was cute.”

“I mean, yeah, but . . .” I didn’t know what else to say without lying, which I didn’t want to do to my best friend’s face, or admitting that I had a thing for Mihai, which I definitely didn’t want to do, either.

Luckily, Noelle didn’t seem to want to hear me talk about him any more than I wanted to talk about him. She held up her hand, squeezing her eyes shut like she was watching a scary movie and couldn’t take the disturbing images flashing across the screen. “Ugh,” she said, “I don’t need the details. Look, I’m not going to pretend it’s not a little weird. But if you like him and he likes you . . . well, I guess there’s nothing I can do about it. Just don’t let it change our friendship, okay? I really couldn’t handle that.”

“It wouldn’t,” I assured her quickly.

She pointed a finger at me, like a stern teacher lecturing a student about her homework. “And *don’t* ever make out in front of me. That would be too gross.” She gave an exaggerated shudder.

I felt a weird tingle in my stomach when she said that, but I shook my head emphatically. “I wouldn’t,” I promised. I wanted to ask her if she thought that Mihai really did like me back, or if he ever talked about me, but I figured that that would fall under the category of changing our friendship, so I bit my tongue and cast around for something I could bring up that would get us away from this uncomfortable subject.

Noelle seemed as eager as I was to move on, but I didn't like the topic she chose to talk about much better. "Did you get a chance to read that biography I gave you?" she asked.

The last thing in the world I cared about just then was reading some book. I decided to be honest. "Why don't I give it back to you? I don't think I'm going to have a chance to read it."

"Why not?"

I shrugged awkwardly. It *had* been very nice of Noelle to lend me the book, and I didn't want to hurt her feelings. "It's not my thing, that's all."

"But it's about gymnastics," Noelle pointed out. "It's about an *Olympic* gymnast who achieved the greatest feat in the history of our sport. How can that not be your 'thing'?"

I had forgotten that when it came to Nadia Comaneci, Noelle could be a little rabid. Once, an announcer had called a modern gymnast the "next Nadia," and Noelle had gotten offended. She said there could never be another one like her. On the other hand, if people ever compared Noelle to Nadia, she would get shy and flustered and say something about how it was only because of her brown hair and brown eyes and Romanian heritage. Still, I knew she was flattered.

"We're supposed to write about a book that relates to our expectations essay, right?" I pointed out. Noelle nodded. "So, I'm sorry, but this story about a gymnast who was found on a playground and was, like, an instant genius and became the best ever doesn't exactly make me feel good about myself. How am I supposed to live up to that?"

"It's not about *living up* to it," Noelle said. "It's about *striving* for it. Don't you think it's better to have high expectations than none at all? If you fall short, fine. At least you achieved something on the way."

"So, you're telling me," I said, "that if you didn't make the Olympics, and had to settle for competing on some college team instead, you'd be okay with that?"

"I wouldn't define that as *settling*."

"But you want the Olympics," I pointed out,

"or else you wouldn't have taken the National team money. If you didn't think you were going to go all the way, you wouldn't have taken that money, right?"

She squirmed a little on her stool. I could tell I was making her uncomfortable, but I stood my ground. If Noelle was going to start making speeches about striving for Nadia Comaneci's perfect tens, then I was going to call her on it. Not everything could be a perfect ten. That was life.

"Sure, I hope to go to the Olympics," Noelle said. "I think about it all the time. I literally dream about it. But that doesn't mean that there aren't many other paths that could make me happy. Don't you feel that way?"

Right now, it was hard for me to think of even one path that would make me happy. If I was at a crossroads, staring at several different paths, then one of them had the Olympic rings at the end of it. I loved my sport, and I loved my team. But gymnastics also meant my mother yelling at me, Mademoiselle Colette tapping me and telling me to straighten up, Dr. Michaels examining my Achilles tendon and reporting that the pain could always come back. And the other paths had . . . what? If not the Olympics, then what?

"What's the real reason you haven't written your essay?" Noelle asked me quietly.

"I told you," I said, "with this injury and—"

Noelle sighed, running her fingernail along a groove in the lacquered wooden counter. "I know English isn't your favorite subject," she said, "but you've always done your homework before. This time, you haven't even bothered to check out the *Great Expectations* movie. That's not like you."

I shrugged. When I'd decided to come over, I'd been sixty percent hoping to run into Mihai and maybe see if he wanted to ride bikes like he'd said, and forty percent hoping, that, if not, I could at least relax with Noelle. There was no percent of me that had been looking for psychoanalysis. "I just can't picture it, you know?" I twirled a long strand of black hair around my finger, until I remembered that it was a habit my mother had forced me to break three years ago.

Noelle seemed to understand that my question hadn't really been directed toward her. She remained quiet as I gathered my thoughts.

"I mean, you seem to know exactly what you expect to happen in five years," I said. "You can visualize the medal, and the crowds, and the tour after the Olympics, and everything. Even when I fake-interview myself—"

I realized too late what I was saying, and glanced at her to find her hiding a smile. "It's okay," she said. "I do that, too, sometimes."

"Anyway," I said, glad my long hair covered the tips of my burning ears, "even when I fake-interview myself, it's like it's happening in a vacuum. I'm talking about things like sweeping all of the events and being an Olympic all-around champion, and yet somehow I don't actually expect those things to happen."

"What *do* you expect to happen?"

"That's the problem," I said, sighing. "That's why I haven't written the essay. I don't know. If I'm totally honest—and God, I can't even believe I'm saying this out loud—I kind of always knew that *you* would win the all-around gold medal. I can picture that better than I can picture me winning it."

Noelle blinked. "Wow," she said. "I don't know what to say."

I waved my hand at her. "You don't have to say anything. I'm only admitting the truth for the first time in my life. I think I'm a really good gymnast, but I don't think I'm as good as you or Britt. Look at how she was able to get that full-in when she was, like, eleven, and I spent months and months on it."

"It's not about how fast you learn stuff, though—" Noelle started to point out, but I cut her off. Now that I was finally laying out the way I felt—the way I'd been feeling for a while, I realized—I didn't want anyone trying to talk me out of it.

"And you know what's the biggest kicker of all?" I asked. "I'm not sure that I *want* to win it. Obviously, if you told me you could hand me that gold medal right now and put me down in history books as the champion, sure, I'd take it. But I don't think I want it the way you do, or even the way Jessie does, or Britt."

Just then, there was a clatter from above us and the sound of shoes pounding down the staircase, and Mihai appeared in the doorway. When he saw me, he smiled.

"Hey, Christina," he said.

And even though I'd shown up hoping to catch a glimpse of Mihai, I suddenly needed to go. I actually knew what I had to write for Ms. Rine's assignment, and I was anxious to get started. It felt like a new beginning in more ways than one.

Nine

By the time school was back in session, I was actually superpsyched for Ms. Rine's class. I'd read the biography of Nadia Comaneci (Noelle was right; it turned out to be really interesting), and finished my book report. I'd also finished my essay about *Great Expectations*.

Okay, so I hadn't read the whole book yet. I had started it, though, which was more than I could say for most books we were assigned in English. I wasn't even upset that my mom still wouldn't let me rent the movie, which was apparently rated R. I'd forgotten how cool it could be just to lose yourself in words, to let your imagination fill in everything instead of relying on someone else's.

Ms. Rine asked everyone to pass their essays up to the front and when I didn't include mine, Noelle turned around to frown at me.

"Don't you have it?" she whispered.

I proudly held up my essay: three pages, double-spaced, that I'd polished just the night before. After dinner, instead of heading down to the basement to practice on the barre like I'd done prior to my injury, or parking myself in front of the TV until my mom told me to go find something to do, I'd booted up the computer in my dad's study and worked on the essay. I hadn't even played my new gymnastics game, though it had been tempting.

"Phew," Noelle said. No kidding, she actually said that. Noelle was so precious sometimes. "Here, hand it up."

"I want to give it to Ms. Rine myself," I said. "I totally slaved over this thing."

So when the bell rang, I hung behind, approaching Ms. Rine's desk once everyone else had cleared out of the room.

"Yes, Christina?" she said.

I held out my report and the essay, which I'd put in a nice folder with a clear cover. "I wanted to make sure you got these," I said, knowing there was no reason why she wouldn't have received them fine if I'd handed them up with everyone else.

She accepted them with a smile. "Wonderful, Christina," she said, flipping the plastic cover back to look over the first page. I felt suddenly self-conscious. During the time I'd been writing the essay, it hadn't really sunk in that she was going to *read* it. Watching her eyes skim over my words, wondering what she was thinking, made my heart race like I was getting set for a huge dismount.

"This looks great," she said. "I can't wait to get into it. You're a very talented writer."

I was sure that it was the kind of thing that English teachers said to all their students, to encourage them to love their subject, but I still flushed. "No, I'm not," I said, and it wasn't even false modesty. I knew that English wasn't really my best class.

"Yes, you are," Ms. Rine said. "Your words have this natural flow to them, almost like they're dancing on the page. It's hard to explain, but believe me, it's rare. You should treasure it as a gift."

"Well, I *am* a dancer," I said, then shook my head. "I mean, a gymnast. I'm a gymnast."

Ms. Rine gently placed my report on the top

of the stack on her desk, almost like she wanted to make sure nothing happened to it. "I know," she said. "Maybe that's why. You're graceful in everything you do, it seems."

I'd been told that before, in ballet and gymnastics. It was always nice to be admired, but for some reason, it meant a lot to me to hear Ms. Rine say it now. I'd never thought of school as a place where I could be particularly graceful. In many of my subjects, I felt clumsy, like I was trying to walk a balance beam wearing weighted boots.

"I've enjoyed your class," I said, and I realized it was true. I wouldn't have said it a month ago, but now I could see that Ms. Rine challenged us to go beyond what we read and think about how those books applied to the world outside the classroom and to our own lives. That was pretty cool, when you really thought about it.

"Thank you," Ms. Rine said. "I believe you're going to like the next book we read, *Little Women*. One of the characters in the book, who's based on the author herself, is a writer."

Okay, I *knew* that one was a movie. I'd seen it before, when I was younger. The youngest sister had been played by that girl who was later in *Bring It*

On, which was one of my favorite movies, because it had a lot of tumbling in it.

I knew I should probably read the book for class before I saw the movie again. "Sounds great," I said.

Noelle was waiting for me out in the hall, although it meant that she'd be pushing it to get to her next class on time. "How'd it go?" she asked.

"She didn't understand why I would do my report on Nadia Comaneci," I said, "when everyone knows Olga Korbut was the superior gymnast."

Noelle's eyes blazed as if I'd insulted her family. "Olga Korbut was amazing, don't get me wrong," she said, "but does Ms. Rine even remember the 1976 Olympics? Let's see, who got the gold medal on the balance beam, with a perfect ten, might I add? Oh, yeah, Nadia. Who won the silver? Olga. I'm not trying to be a hater, I'm just saying."

"Hater?" I repeated incredulously. "Oh, my God, please never use that word again. I'm totally kidding. Ms. Rine didn't say anything against any past gymnasts, so you can calm down."

"Oh." A second later, Noelle giggled, nudging me with her elbow. "You hater."

For a while now, I'd actually kind of felt like a hater about everything myself. But it was kind of ironic that Noelle would use that word to describe me, even as a joke. Because for the first time, I was feeling like there wasn't a whole lot to hate in this world, not even *Great Expectations* or writing essays.

As my mom had told me they would, Mo and Cheng talked to me about adding something really cool to my bar routine to stand out at the Invitational. Well, Mo mostly did the talking, with Cheng nodding in a couple of places.

I was really excited about it. Mo's first idea had been to use the Arabian I had been practicing on the floor and incorporate it into a new mount or dismount, but of course those were both parts of the routine that I wasn't able to work on because of my Achilles tendon. So instead, she suggested I add a Tkachev to a Gienger release combination, which would boost my difficulty level by a lot.

"But do you really think I can pull that off?" I'd asked Mo.

"Do you?" she responded.

I'd done both a Tkachev and a Gienger in my bar routine before, but never together. It would be difficult to figure out how to connect them fluidly without any break in my swing. In a Tkachev, you swung forward, letting go of the bar to sail backward over it and catch it between your straddled legs. In order to add a Gienger to the end of that, I wouldn't get a full swing on the bar before I would have to let go again, this time twisting in the air before I caught it again. It was going to be insane.

The downside was that this practice separated me from the rest of the team even more. Whereas before, bars had at least been one place where we could all work out together, I now spent some of my bars practice working on this new release combination over the foam pit, to protect myself in case I fell. Mo reminded me that it was better to belly-flop when falling from bars, though it often looked worse to people in the audience. Even without an Achilles tendon injury to worry about, you could do a lot more damage to yourself trying to recover in midair and land on your feet than you would if you just gave in to the fall.

I took Mo's advice, and was on what felt like my eightieth repetition when Britt got called out of practice. That was weird. But, I had a lot to focus on, since I had yet to complete the two skills in a way that would earn me points in a competition: with no pause in between, and without a break in form.

In fact, I'd only caught the bar both times I was supposed to on, like, four of the attempts I'd made so far.

And yet I didn't feel intimidated by it. Instead, I felt energized, ready to nail this skill. All the worrying I'd done about whether I'd go to the Olympics or not, where I'd be in five years, didn't matter. All that mattered was where I was now, and the sense of accomplishment I'd feel when I finally learned this skill.

I was concentrating so intensely that I'd forgotten about Britt's uncharacteristic absence until she returned, visibly shaking.

"What's wrong?" Jessie asked, crossing over to her. Noelle stopped in midswing and jumped down from the high bar, staring at Britt.

"It's my grandmother," Britt said. She started crying.

Generally, Britt was the one who made all of us laugh, who kept things light, figuring out ways to turn even the most tedious stretching exercise into something hilarious. So I wasn't used to seeing her like this. I didn't know what to do. I'd climbed out of the foam pit and was standing helplessly by the bars, not sure if she needed a hug. Even if she did, I didn't know if she'd want one from me, since we hadn't exactly started out as the best of friends, although I thought we got along pretty well now.

"What happened?" Noelle asked. Her gaze searched mine for an instant, and I could tell she was thinking the same thing I was. *Had Britt's grandmother died?*

Britt's grandmother, Asta, had homeschooled her since she was, like, eight. They were closer than most grandmothers and granddaughters were. When my dad's mother passed away a couple of years ago, I'd been sad, and it had been hard to hear my dad tell stories about her and realize that I would never know her like that, because we hadn't had the time. But because I hadn't known her that well, I wasn't devastated. Britt would be, though. She spent more time with her grandmother than she did with her parents.

"She had a stroke," Britt said. "She's in the hospital right now. My mom is waiting outside. I have to go."

It was a testament to how out of it Britt was that she scooped up Noelle's gym bag. Jessie gently slid the strap off Britt's shoulder and handed her her own bag. Then she gave Britt a long hug, which is what I knew we'd all wanted to do from the moment we'd heard the news, but it definitely felt right for Jessie to be the one to give it to her. It could be hard to read Britt. She wasn't really a touchy-feely kind of person. She and Jessie were tight, though, so it made me feel better to know that Jessie at least could be there for her like that.

"I hope everything is okay," I said, squeezing her shoulder as she passed by. I didn't know what else to say. I couldn't even imagine how badly she might be freaking out just then.

If something happened to my family, I wouldn't know what to do with myself. I realized that I'd never truly apologized to my mother for Christmas, and I vowed to do that. She might've been frustrating, but I knew she just wanted to do the best for me, and she was my mother. She was the only one I had.

Ten

I wanted to talk to my mom about everything, but I wasn't sure how to begin. The time never seemed right. It felt like she was constantly busy—mostly doing stuff for me, which caused the seed of guilt in my stomach to grow exponentially until it was like a full-grown watermelon.

I was busy, too, working on my new skill at the gym. Britt's grandmother was still in the hospital, although she was doing much better. Britt had missed some practice, but she didn't seem to worry about whether it would affect her performance at the Invitational.

* * *

When Dr. Michaels had first told me it would be six weeks until he'd be evaluating me again to tell me if I was ready to go back to full-time training, it had seemed like forever. And yet, now the day was here, and my mom and I were sitting in his waiting room, after I'd been put through several different scans of my foot and leg, hoping to find out the verdict.

I tried to take a page out of Britt's book and not worry about it. I'd done everything I could to take pressure off my Achilles, and I wasn't feeling those twinges of pain anymore. There were two weeks left until the Invitational, which should have been time enough to get most of my skills back. It would have to be.

So, when the nurse called us back into the exam room, I was taking deep, steady breaths, and I even managed to give my mom a wide smile.

"What?" she asked, almost mistrustfully.

Can't I just smile sometimes? I wanted to ask, but I really didn't want to start a fight with her, especially when I was still feeling bad about the last one. "It's exciting," I said. "Soon I'll be able to go back to gymnastics full-time!"

Now it was her turn to smile; hers looked more

like one of relief than one of excitement. "Yes," she said, "but don't—"

At that moment, Dr. Michaels came into the room. He was wearing glasses, and they actually made him look younger than before, if that was possible.

"How's our little gymnast doing?" he asked, winking at me. "Anxious to get back to it, I would imagine."

I nodded emphatically, and he laughed.

"Okay, well, let's check it out," he said. He slid a large, plasticky sheet out of a manila folder and secured it to a backlit clipboard. I could see the outline of my ankle, my toes and foot, and the beginning of my calf. He stared at the image for a few moments. I tried to read his face. Was it bad news? Did everything look okay? I was even more nervous than when Ms. Rine had had my essay in her hands. Those were my words, my feelings on paper, but this was my entire future.

"Well?" my mother demanded impatiently. For once I was kind of glad that she was being pushy. The anticipation was killing me. "What do you see?"

Dr. Michaels smiled up at us. "It looks much better," he said. "I can see that you stayed off it and rested like we discussed. My favorite patients are the ones who listen."

I hadn't realized how stiff my back was until I let my shoulders drop as I sighed with relief. "I haven't done a single dismount or tumbling pass or vault in the past six weeks," I said. "I never thought I would miss vault, but I kind of do."

Dr. Michaels laughed. "I hear you. Well, Christina, the good news is that your tendon seems to be healing nicely, and I think you're going to have an amazing career ahead of you."

That should've made me beam with pleasure, but I was focusing on the way he said *good news*, as though there were some of the other kind as well. Apparently, my mom picked up on this, too, because she said sharply, "The *good* news?"

"It's very good news," Dr. Michaels said. "But unfortunately, I'm not sure that I would recommend competing with this injury just yet. I wouldn't want you to undo all of the great work you've put into getting your body healthy."

I really hadn't seen that coming. I had thought, worst-case scenario, that I just wouldn't be at the top of my form because of the time off, but it had never occurred to me that I wouldn't be competing at all. A sudden image flashed through my mind, of me clapping up in the stands while Britt and Jessie and Noelle flipped their way over vaults and across the beam. I might have admitted to Noelle that I wasn't sure I wanted that ultimate prize—the Olympic gold medal—quite as much as she did, but I knew I wanted *this*. I wanted to be at that Invitational, and not as a spectator.

"I have to compete!" I protested, but my mom was already talking over me.

"What about a cortisone shot?" she asked, as she'd asked Mo at the very beginning of this whole mess. "I heard that last year's World champion was competing with a wrist issue that she had to get cortisone shots for."

Dr. Michaels shook his head, shooting it down the way Mo had six weeks earlier. "That helps with the pain," he said, "but it doesn't really treat the problem. Christina, are you still feeling any pain?"

"Not really," I said. Maybe this would be all he needed to know in order to change his mind. *Oh, well, that's a different story, then!* he'd say. *Good luck at the Invitational!*

I might have been lucky in lots of ways, but right now my luck seemed like it wasn't enough.

Dr. Michaels nodded with satisfaction, noting my answer down on one of his charts, he didn't reverse his decision.

"That's only your *recommendation*, though," my mother said.

Now it was Dr. Michaels's turn to look a little impatient. It was the first time I'd ever seen him betray any kind of emotion other than a cheerful professionalism. "Of course," he said, "if you discuss it with Mo, and she feels like Christina can compete, that is certainly your prerogative. But yes, it's my recommendation as a doctor that she not stress her body too much. I'd hate to see her in this office again." He gave me a small smile. "Not that it's not always a pleasure to see you," he said.

I tried to return his smile, to let him know that I understood what he meant. It really wasn't his fault that any of this was happening; he was only trying to be a good doctor. But I felt frozen, unable to do anything but sit there on that exam table, my mind racing. No Invitational. That meant that I wouldn't be down there on the floor with my teammates, I wouldn't be on TV, I wouldn't have the chance to be one of the first Junior girls ever to compete at the event.

My mother made a rude sound that wasn't too far from one of Britt's snorts. I could already guess that her mind was racing, too, thinking of ways to convince Mo to let me compete despite what Dr. Michaels had said. "Come on, Christina," she said. "Let's go home."

She didn't wait for me but headed right out the door, her heels clicking on the linoleum all the way to the front desk.

Dr. Michaels gave me a sympathetic look, as though telling me to hang in there. "I'm sorry I didn't have better news," he said, "but, Christina, as an athlete, your biggest responsibility is to take care of your instrument, your body. I know it can be hard to miss this opportunity. Believe me, I know. But in the long run, this really is the best decision."

"Is that what happened to you?" I asked. "Why you didn't go to the Olympics?"

Dr. Michaels laughed, as if he hadn't expected me to be so direct. "Not exactly," he said. "I wasn't really Olympic material. I had an amazing college career, and was able to save on student loans while studying medicine, which is what I'd always known I wanted to do. So I can't complain."

"You didn't always want to be a gymnast?" I

asked in disbelief. He'd trained for hours a day like me and somehow it wasn't his entire world? How could someone who had devoted as many hours a day to training as I did now *not* have that be their entire world? It made no sense.

"As something fun to do and a way to be a part of a team, sure," he said. "As a means to keep myself healthy and challenge myself, absolutely. But that's what gymnastics was for me: a means. Not necessarily an end. Do you see what I'm saying?"

I thought back to the essay I'd written for Ms. Rine. "I think I do," I said.

In the car on the way home, my mom drummed her fingernails on the steering wheel, fiddling with the heater dial until hot air was blasting in my face. Even though it had been cold outside, it was starting to get too warm in the car. I hated the way the heat dried my eyes out. I closed the vents in front of me.

"If you don't want it on, just say so," my mom said, reaching over to turn the heat off.

"I thought you wanted it on," I said.

"But when you close the vents," she snapped, "you make the heat on my side blast twice as strong. So I *can't* keep the heat on, now, can I?"

I didn't know why she was getting so upset about such a stupid thing. We were both still wearing our coats, and having the warm air fill the car for the first ten minutes had made it nice and cozy.

I was almost scared to venture another word, but I did want to apologize for what had happened on Christmas, even though that had been weeks ago. Maybe that was why my mother was angry with me, because she'd never gotten over that fight. "Mom, I—" I began, but she cut me off.

"You shouldn't have been running around with your friends so much," she said. "Maybe then you would be ready to compete."

Running around with my friends? It's not like we'd spent time jumping down the stairs, me hopping on my one bad foot the whole way. They'd come over once to hang out, and I'd gone over to Noelle's house. We'd sat practically the whole time.

When I told my mom that, though, she raised her eyebrows. "You're always complaining that you never have time to see your friends and that you have to wake up so early," she said. "I'm only saying that now, you got a little break, and see what it got you. You're going to have to work extra hard if you want to make up for this in time for Nationals this summer."

I felt tears smarting in my eyes, and I turned toward the window so she wouldn't see them. That was so unfair. I hadn't gone to gym one day and said, "Gee, I think I'll fake a big old injury so that I can relax. Somehow I'll rig the test results, so that even the doctor thinks it's real. All so I can derail everything my mother and I have slaved for over the years."

The words were building in my head, and they had to spill over, the way the tears were starting to run down my cheeks. "I feel like Cinderella," I said. "Wash the dishes, clean the floors. Except with me, it's, like, Nail that dismount, get more height on your leaps."

"So I guess that puts me in the role of the evil stepmother, hmm?" my mother said.

That wasn't what I'd meant, but now that she'd said it, I felt unable to correct her. Or at least unwilling to.

"I'm so evil I pay half a house payment every month to make sure you get the best training possible," she said. I wanted to make a smart-aleck comment about how *she* didn't work for that money, since it was my dad who earned the big bucks, but even I knew that that would have been pushing it too far.

"I'm so evil I wake up at five so I can get *you* up at five thirty every morning, and I make sure you have a balanced breakfast. Then I drive you to the gym, where I hang out until I have to drive you and your friends to school. Then I do it all over that afternoon, only now I help out at the gym, just to pass the time while I wait for you to finish your practice. Do you know how much time I spend *waiting* for you?"

"Then stop," I said. "Take me out of gymnastics. I don't care."

But of course, I *did* care. I might not have been the best gymnast in the world, and I sometimes got frustrated when I wasn't doing as well as I thought I could, but I really did love the sport. That was the part I forgot sometimes when I started thinking about how I'd transitioned from ballet to gymnastics. My mom had moved me to tumbling classes because I'd said it was more fun, and I wanted to do that more than dressing up in tutus and putting on recitals. I'd always loved gymnastics.

"Maybe I will," she said, "and then I can have a life."

As soon as we got home, my mom barked at me to go up to my room. I had been planning on escaping up there anyway. I couldn't believe I'd started out the day ready to apologize to my mother and try to make it right between us, and now I was angrier than ever at her. I was already upset about Dr. Michaels's news and the fact that I wouldn't be competing at the Invitational. Couldn't she focus on comforting me, instead of making me feel worse about it?

I slammed my bedroom door, trying to channel some of my anger into that one satisfying motion. But it was still there, pent up, in every inch of my body, and I searched around my room for something to take it out on. I almost wished I could do an entire floor routine right here, but there wasn't enough space . . . and I wasn't supposed to be tumbling on my Achilles tendon, anyway.

I saw the stack of *Flip for Gymnastics* magazines on my desk, left there from when Noelle and Jessie and Britt had come over. The magazines were in perfect condition; my mom didn't even like me to bend the cover back behind the pages, because she said that ruined the collectibility of them. I'd never understood why she was so hung up on that kind of thing, because I wasn't planning on selling them, and you could order back issues online.

Before I could second-guess myself, I grabbed a pair of scissors and sat down at my desk. I opened up the first magazine, one with the European champion from two years ago on the cover, and started cutting.

At first, I hastily slashed around images I liked, without looking at the other side of the page to see if there was something even better there. I cut crudely around each figure, without worrying about following the lines of the body too closely. But after a few minutes had passed, I felt my breathing even out, and a picture formed in my head of an art project I could do with all of these clippings. I began to cut more carefully, paying attention to the images I wanted, and snipping with such small motions that I had to take a break to rest my cramped hand.

I really loved taking on this kind of project, but it was hard to find the time when I was so busy with gymnastics. I wondered if that was what my mother had meant when she'd said she didn't have a life. Maybe there was something like this, something that she liked to do but couldn't because she had to wait around for me at gym and cook me healthy meals all the time. I'd spent the last few weeks questioning my commitment to this Olympic dream, wondering if it was worth all of the time and energy and achiness and exhaustion. My mom had always seemed driven toward that goal, even more than I was. It had never occurred to me that she might have had her doubts, too.

Eleven

If my mom and I had held out any hope that Mo might override Dr. Michaels's advice, it was quickly dashed when we met with her the next day.

"I think that good idea," Mo said when we'd finished reporting to her what Dr. Michaels had said.

"Even though it means she'll miss the Invitational completely?" my mom said incredulously. "You told me it was a huge honor for Christina to be invited to compete at that meet. And now you want her to miss it?"

My mother looked as tired as I felt. The night before, I'd stayed up later than my usual bedtime clipping pictures from my magazines and laying them out on my floor to see how I might want to place them. I'd had to put myself to bed because my mother hadn't come up to check on me. In the morning, she'd stared at the cutout gymnasts leaping and flipping and twisting across my floor, and taken in the now-shredded magazines on my desk, but she hadn't said anything.

"Well," Mo said, "there might be way around that. I propose we make Christina bars specialist."

"Bars specialist?" my mom repeated. "What does that mean?"

I had an idea, and I'm sure my mother did, too, since she'd watched every single televised competition for the past three years, but I figured that she just wanted to hear Mo explain it. A bars specialist was a gymnast who competed only on the bars, because she was thought to have some kind of special ability or talent for that one event. Even at competitions as huge as the Olympics, it was becoming pretty common for teams to have at least one specialist, usually somebody who could score out of this world on an event like vault, where other gymnasts tended to struggle, but who wasn't a contender for the all-around.

It was that last part that my mother wasn't happy about. "So she won't be eligible for an all-around medal?"

Mo gave my mother a pointed look. "A medal on bars better than nothing," she said. "Christina will do only because she has hurt tendon. When she get better, she can go back to four events."

My mother still looked doubtful. It was obvious that she wanted Mo's go-ahead for me to return to full training, with dismounts and tumbling and everything. It was equally obvious, to me, that Mo wasn't going to give her that. I would have to take what I could get, and I decided I'd much rather go to the Invitational and do one bars routine than sit up in the stands.

"Sounds great," I said. "Will they let me do that?"

Mo nodded. "I will process paperwork with USAG," she said. "With new skill, you have chance of getting very good score."

I felt my spirits lift for the first time since Dr. Michaels had dropped that bad news about my injury. Sure, it wasn't the result I'd hoped for at the start of this ordeal, but I was excited to show off my Tkachev to Gienger combination, which was really coming along in practice. Even though I was a Junior and would be doing only one routine, I thought I had a shot at making it onto the television broadcast with something that cool.

My mom seemed to think that things needed to be all or nothing, but I remembered what Dr. Michaels had said the day before, when I'd asked him about the Olympics. Gymnastics didn't have to be that way. The sport could give you a lot if you let it. You had to be open to the opportunities that presented themselves and not worry too much about the ones that didn't.

The weekend after my appointment with the doctor, Mihai called to ask if I wanted to come over on Sunday and go for a bike ride with him. When I ran the idea by my mom, I did it with a defiant tilt of my chin, waiting for her to call me out for the criticism she'd given me earlier, that now that I was injured I was letting myself coast. There was no way she was going to let me go hang out with Mihai, even if it *was* for exercise, a point that I made sure to emphasize so she wouldn't get all weird and protective about my spending time with a boy.

Oddly, though, my mom didn't say no. She

picked up her car keys as if she had no choice in the matter, and told me that she'd come to Noelle's parents' store to pick me up in a couple of hours. I almost wanted to say never mind, forget it, because I was so freaked out by her lack of a response after she'd been so vocal earlier about my supposed slacking off.

Almost. Then again, here was my chance to see Mihai, who I'd liked for years and who I was starting to think might like me back.

When I showed up at the store, Mihai answered the door. I was kind of relieved, since it would've been awkward to see Noelle this particular day. I assumed she knew that I was coming over to see Mihai, because she'd had to give him my phone number, but still.

"You ready?" he asked. I nodded. He led me to the shed where they kept their bikes locked up. He wheeled Noelle's bike out to the sidewalk and propped it on its kickstand while he helped me buckle Noelle's helmet on my head.

"Are you sure she doesn't mind me using her stuff?" I asked.

"She said no," he responded, "although she told me not to kiss you while you were riding her bike.

She said that would be completely disgusting."

He was already climbing on his bike, so I couldn't see his face to tell if he was serious. Thankfully, that also meant that he couldn't see my burning cheeks.

"You're going to have to pedal faster than you do on that stationary bike if you want to keep up with me," he said. "Let's see if you can do it!"

And with that, he took off, leaving me still standing over my bike. I placed one sneaker on a pedal and pushed off with my other foot, following Mihai down the street. It was a few moments before I felt steady enough to start building up some speed, but once I did, it was exhilarating. Even though the air was cold and chapped my lips, there was something really awesome about the feeling of coasting down a hill, going faster and faster when your feet weren't even on the pedals anymore.

We biked around for twenty minutes without talking. Mihai led me up and down quiet streets I'd never even known existed. He seemed to sense it when I started to tire, because he pulled in to the parking lot of a coffee shop and stopped his bike. "How about some hot chocolate?" he asked.

I nodded gratefully. We walked up and ordered;

I tried to offer to pay for my own with some allowance money I'd brought with me, but Mihai just waved me off. There were no tables or chairs, so we sat down on the curb. I blew on my hot chocolate, trying to cool it down a little bit before taking a cautious sip.

"Noelle told me about the Invitational," he said. "You're only going to be competing on bars?"

I nodded. "Yeah, I got the okay from Dr. Michaels to work on my dismount for my bar routine, which is the only high-impact skill I've done in a while. Luckily, my mount is only a glide kip, so it doesn't put a lot of stress on my Achilles."

Mihai laughed. "I was following you until you lapsed into gymnastics-ese. Just because I live with a diehard gymnast doesn't mean I've picked up all the lingo."

"But you picked up the love of *Riverdance* music," I said teasingly. "It's a fancy way of saying I jump on the low bar and then pull myself up into a handstand. . . . You know what? It doesn't matter. I'm really excited to compete on bars at the Invitational, actually. It would've been cool if I could've done all four events, obviously, but I don't know. Maybe this is better."

"What do you mean?"

I shrugged. "Less pressure," I said. "I get to focus on making one routine completely awesome and don't have to worry about the rest."

"That's a good way to look at it," Mihai said. He was staring out into the distance, as though watching something far away, but when I looked in that direction I couldn't see anything particularly interesting. There was only the side of an old building that had some graffiti of fists painted on it with red spray paint. The sign on the roof proclaimed that it was a boxing gym of some kind, which I guess made sense.

"I can't imagine how you and Noelle and the other girls do it," he said. "I go crazy if I have a test coming up at school or my dad's counting on me to fix something at the store. I don't think I could take the kind of stress you guys are under all the time."

There was a blue-and-white-striped candy wrapper by my foot, and every time I tapped it with my toe, it made a satisfying crinkling noise. I did that over and over, taking sips of my hot chocolate in between, while I thought about what Mihai was saying.

"That's what I realized," I said. "You can't think about everything that's coming up. Sometimes you just have to think about right now."

Mihai chuckled. "Okay, that sounds totally deep, but I have no clue how it relates to gymnastics."

I kicked the candy wrapper out of the way, watching it bounce toward the gutter. "Like when you take a test," I said. "It seems like the end of the world, like nothing else could possibly exist after you take this one thing you've been studying for forever. Right?"

"Yeah," Mihai said, as if he were seeing something clearly for the first time. I could practically hear the lightbulb go on over his head. It encouraged me, so I turned to face him, getting more excited now.

"But that's not true," I said. "The test is only one step on this long road toward college, which is a road toward getting a job, which is a road toward . . . the rest of your life, I guess. It's the same with gymnastics. I was all worked up about this Invitational, but the truth is that it's only one competition in the grand scheme of things, and I'll be back to competing on all four events in no time. Even gymnastics isn't really the end, although I always thought it was. Does that make sense?"

"Total sense," Mihai said.

I took a sip of my hot chocolate, which created a trail of warmth leading from my throat to my stomach.

Before I knew what was happening, Mihai leaned over and gave me a quick kiss on the cheek. It wasn't anything huge—a brief brush of his lips, so soft it almost felt unreal—but it left a lingering feeling of warmth even greater than the one my hot chocolate had left.

"What was that for?" I asked. I couldn't stop the smile from growing on my face.

"You're so cool," he said. "That's all."

We sat on that curb for another twenty minutes, finishing our hot chocolate and talking about everything from musicals (I liked them; Mihai didn't) to school (Mihai's favorite subject was science, I learned) to *Riverdance* (Mihai admitted that he did actually kind of like watching those people dance). By the time we got back on our bikes and headed toward his parents' store, I was thinking that it couldn't have been a more awesome day.

It didn't even matter if it was officially a date or

not. It didn't have to be all or nothing. It could just be what it was, and it happened to have been completely and utterly perfect.

My mom was silent on the drive home, which was fine by me, since the last thing I wanted was for her to snipe at me about slacking off again and ruin my good mood. But once we got in the house, I couldn't stand it. I didn't want things to be weird anymore between my mom and me. A part of me wanted to avoid a fight for as long as this warm feeling from Mihai's kiss lasted, but I also didn't want another minute to pass before telling my mom how I felt.

Instead of retreating to my bedroom like I would've normally done, I went and found her in the kitchen, where she was starting to heat up a pot of stew on the stove.

"I'm sorry—" I began, but my mother cut me off.

"No, I'm sorry," she said.

I blinked, surprised. I totally hadn't expected this reaction. I mean, yeah, she'd yelled at me a few times, but I'd been a full-on brat.

My mother dried her hands on a dish towel, although this looked more like a nervous action than anything else, since her hands didn't seem to be wet. What did *she* have to be nervous about? I was the one who was about to throw myself at her feet and beg forgiveness.

"I went into your room because I wanted to see if you'd written anything in your diary about Mihai, now that he's calling the house and asking you over. I know it was wrong, and as soon as I was in there I changed my mind and decided I was going to respect your privacy. But then I saw your essay, sitting on your desk, and I couldn't help it. I sat down and I read it."

For a moment, I was literally speechless. She'd read my *essay*? I fought to remember every single word I'd put in there, to see if any of it had been incriminating.

"I had no idea you felt that way," she said. "When you talked about wanting to be happy above everything else, it really struck a chord with me. That's *my* goal for you, too. And all that you said about everyone's expectations . . . I had no idea I was pushing you that hard. I thought we were committed to the same goal, and I guess I got a little blinded along the way by all the possibilities for your future. But that doesn't mean that it's more important to me that you win a gold medal than that you're happy, Christina, I hope you know that."

I wasn't thrilled about my mother's going into my room and reading my stuff without my permission, but I guessed if it helped her to see my perspective, that had to be a good thing. "I was such a brat on Christmas," I said. "You give me everything, and I threw it back in your face, and I am so, so sorry. . . ."

She shook her head. "Sometimes I get you what *I* want you to have, rather than what you want. I really don't mean to do that, and I hope you'll let me know if I do it again."

She gave me a stern look, swatting me playfully with the dish towel. "Perhaps next time with a bit less attitude, though. What do you think?"

I nodded gratefully. "I was like one of those brides on that show you watch," I said. "Call me Daughterzilla, or Christmaszilla. I don't know. The point is, I promise not to do it again!"

My mother gathered me up in a hug. She smelled like a mixture of chicken broth and her usual floral perfume, but somehow the scent was nice. She started talking while she was still holding me, and the rumble of her voice in my ear as she pressed me to her chest was comforting, too.

"I wanted to say some of this to you earlier," she said. "I didn't mean for you to think that I was mad at you after you got injured. I was frustrated with the situation. I was seeing all that we'd worked for—all that *you'd* worked for—may be put in jeopardy and it broke my heart to think that you might not get to compete at that Invitational. I didn't know how to express any of that. But then I read your essay, and I realized that if you could be brave enough to put all of your feelings into words, then I could be, too. I'm sorry if I've been too hard on you."

I wanted to tell her that it was okay, that I understood. Not that I didn't get angry sometimes that she was always on me about my toe point and my layout position and my difficulty level. But I'd done a lot of thinking about what my mom had said to my dad during that overheard dinner conversation, and about what she'd said to me in the car. It was only me and her most of the time, and it had to be tough for her to take responsibility for my gymnastics and my future. If she went overboard sometimes, well, I guess it was to be expected.

I let my dad off the hook, because when he came into town, everything was all fancy dinners and presents from out-of-town destinations. But on the other hand, he wasn't around that much. It had been my mother who'd taken me to see Dr. Michaels, and my mother who had really had to talk to Mo about what we were going to do about my injury. My dad's full-time job was being a surgeon and a scientist and a speaker. My mom's full-time job was me.

I wanted to tell her all of this, but I also didn't want to make her sad. I knew that she missed my dad, too. So instead I squeezed her hard in a hug, trying to let her know with my arms and my body that I appreciated everything she did for me.

Twelve

Of course, on the long drive to the Invitational in New Orleans, my mom did have a couple questions for me, like why I'd cut up my magazines (she was a little upset, but not as much as I'd thought she would be once I explained what I was going to do with the pictures) and whether or not Mihai was my boyfriend.

The radio was on, but Noelle was sitting in the backseat, so I knew she could totally hear us. "*Mom,*" I hissed. "No, he's not my boyfriend."

Even though Noelle and I had talked about my crush on Mihai, I didn't want her thinking that I was dating Mihai and hadn't told her. And it really wasn't true. Yes, we'd shared a kiss, and yes, I still liked him, but we were *not* going out. After the Invitational, well . . . maybe we'd see how we felt. In the meantime, it was nice just to know that there was someone out there who might be thinking of me, and to think about him from time to time and glow inside.

I'd hoped we would have some time to see the sights once we were in New Orleans, but as soon as we got there, we had to register and check in and do all these other official-type things. We did get gym bags with the details of the meet printed on them, and the bags were filled with goodies like USAG pens, red, white, and blue scrunchies, and a DVD of Invitational highlights from the past.

After we'd checked in, Mo led us deeper into the arena. "Do you girls want to see floor?" Mo asked us, waggling her eyebrows a little bit. It was strange to see Mo be goofy like that. Britt started giggling right there, and Mo seemed to know that this was directed at her, although she didn't appear to mind.

It was good to see Britt laugh again. The past week had been hard: her grandmother had just gotten out of the hospital and was staying with Britt's parents for now. The only sign that she'd had a stroke, Britt said, was that it was a little harder for her to get around than it used to be. Her left side still had some numbness, and so she had to use a cane. Britt's grandmother was so lively and interesting that I think it had stunned Britt to see her actually seeming . . . well, *old*.

Once we'd recovered from the sight of Mo looking like a cartoon character, of course we all were eager to see the competition floor. So, we reached into our gym bags for the ID badges on their re-white-and-blue lanyards we were supposed to wear around our necks and followed Mo through a set of double doors.

I'll never forget the feeling of stepping into that huge arena. The ceiling was so high there were rafters and catwalks up there I could barely even make out. And the seats for the crowd went almost all the way to the top. I remembered reading online that they were expecting more than 15,000 fans for the event. I couldn't believe there would be that many people watching *me*.

I could tell by the way Noelle looked around, her eyes wide, that she was thinking the same thing. "Wow," she breathed.

"This place is *sick*," Britt said. "Can we get up on the podium?"

Mo smiled. "You are four of best Junior gymnast in country," she said. "I say get on the podium."

The Nationals had been on a large scale like this, too, with the podium and everything, so it wasn't like we were totally new to the experience. But that hadn't been an international event—at this Invitational, we'd be competing against some of the best gymnasts from Russia, Romania, China, Bulgaria . . . It was insane. Noelle and I had competed at that USA vs. the World event, but that had been more of an exhibition, which meant that it had a ton of camera-friendly decorations like plastic potted palm trees everywhere (it had been held in San Jose), but it hadn't felt as *official*, somehow.

At big meets like this, the equipment was often put on top of a kind of podium that was like a stage built into the middle of the floor to give some extra drama to the competition. The first time I'd competed on one of these at Nationals, I wasn't prepared for how it really did make things feel a little different. There was a bit of extra spring in the floor, for example, I swear to God.

The podium also had the effect of making the

sidelines feel more separate, a place where gymnasts could keep their muscles warm and wait for their scores and talk more freely with their coaches. As Britt jumped up onto the podium, I stayed put to enjoy the feeling of being down on the main floor for another minute.

"This is so awesome," Jessie said. "I've never competed at a meet like this before."

I'd forgotten that she hadn't ever competed at Nationals, although she'd been up in the stands cheering us on.

"I'm going to make a fool of myself," she said, so low I almost didn't hear her.

I put my arm around her shoulders. "No, you're not," I said. "You're going to be great. We all are."

"We're going to rock this competition," Noelle said, grinning.

"They won't remember that Senior Elites are competing," I added. That might have been stretching it a bit; it was an Olympic year, after all. Everyone was going to be watching to see who we would be sending to represent our country and who might lead us to a team medal.

"Hey!" Britt called from on top of the podium.

"You guys look shorter than ever down there, I hope you know. Get your butts up here!"

Jessie and I climbed up, with Noelle following on the little stairs that connected the elevated platform to the ground level. I'd always watched gymnasts on TV jump up and down off the podium in a way that looked so casual and cool, as if they'd been doing it all their lives and it was no big deal. I kind of wanted to have that same effortless swagger.

I knew that Noelle would play it safe, because she would be worried that she might roll her ankle hopping down from the thing and ruin her entire competition. That was just the way her mind worked.

We joined Britt in the middle of the blue carpet, which looked fresh and ready for some awesome tumbling. I felt a slight pang that I wouldn't be dancing on it, but ignored it and smiled at my teammates.

"You know what this calls for," I said.

"What?" Jessie asked, but from the way Britt's eyes lit up, I could tell that she knew.

"One . . ." she counted down.

"Two . . ." Noelle said.

"Three!" I yelled. And then we all cupped our hands around our mouths and shouted up to the very top of the nosebleed seats, "*Texas Twisters!*"

"*Forever!*" I added. The word echoed throughout the arena. I couldn't wait for the competition to start, so we could show everyone that Texas truly wasn't a state you wanted to mess with, even in gymnastics.

At the American Invitational, there were two days of competition for the Junior Elites. Gymnasts vied for the all-around medals on the first day, which also served as the qualifying day for the event finals, which were held on day two.

I was fortunate that we were on bars first, which meant that I could get my one event out of the way. Even though my Tkachev-Gienger combination had been a little shakier than I'd have liked, at least I didn't fall, and my score was high enough to qualify me as one of the eight gymnasts who'd be moving on to the event finals the next day.

After finishing bars, we moved to beam. I helped my teammates stretch on the sidelines, by holding their ankles while they bent forward in splits; I made sure that they couldn't lift their legs even a millimeter off the ground to cheat.

Jessie was first up on the beam; we all clapped

to cheer her on. "Come on, Jess!" Britt shouted. "You can do it!" Because she was Britt, she yelled that last bit in a funny accent. I saw the tiniest crack of a smile on Jessie's face before she got the signal that the judges were ready for her and gave her salute.

Once she was on the beam, Britt and Noelle made a show of going back to their own stretches. It might have seemed like they didn't care, but I knew that wasn't the case. Gymnastics is a strange sport, in that it's about you up there all by yourself, but it's about being part of a team at the same time. I knew that it could be really hard to focus if you dwelled too much on what other people were doing, even your own teammates. I could watch Jessie, but that's because I was done for the day.

She had a solid routine, landing her tricky sheep jump with a solid *thwack* of her feet on the beam. The sheep jump looks pretty easy, but you can't see the beam before your feet come down, which actually makes it fairly hard. Jessie dismounted, taking only the tiniest step on her landing. I clapped, and then the other girls joined in.

"Go, Jess!" Britt said, giving her a high five as she ran down the steps from the podium.

Jessie grinned. "I know my score won't be that great," she said, "since my difficulty level isn't as high as some of the other girls' here. But that felt good!"

When her score came, she was right: it wasn't as high as that of the Ukrainian girl who'd gone before her, throwing what seemed like every trick in the Code of Points. But Jessie's score was still totally respectable, and the highest she'd ever gotten in an Elite competition.

Noelle was up next on the beam. She got through her routine flawlessly. There was one arabesque she'd been practicing down on the side-lines where she bent forward until her torso was parallel to the beam, with her arms held out grace-fully at her sides. Then she stretched one leg behind her until it formed a completely straight line per-pendicular to the beam. It took my breath away. In a weird way, I was glad I was getting to watch this competition instead of participate in it, since I'd never truly gotten to watch my teammates before. I trained alongside them every day, but it wasn't like I had the chance to be *impressed.* And yet, that was exactly what I was feeling now.

By the time Noelle finished her routine, I had no doubt that her score would be very high. Even the Ukrainian girl had had a couple of tiny bobbles on the beam, while Noelle had seemed perfect. But gymnastics is a subjective sport; you never know what the judges will think. So when Noelle's score came in as high as we'd all expected it to, Jessie and Mo and I all enveloped her in a hug.

Britt shot Noelle a distracted smile. Although I knew she was as happy for Noelle as the rest of us were, she was up next, and so she had to maintain her focus. She'd told us before the competition that she was dedicating all of her routines to her grandmother, who was doing much better but hadn't been up to making the trip to New Orleans, and was watching the competition on TV. I knew that Britt was hoping they would show at least one of her routines, although with only three hours devoted to the broadcast and so many gymnasts competing, not to mention all of the fluff the stations put in the program pre-Olympics to hype up the contenders for those games, it was possible it wouldn't happen.

Everyone in the arena was watching her, though, as she mounted the beam with her powerful punch front. It was a dramatic mount in which she ran onto the springboard and did a tucked front flip directly onto the beam. The crowd cheered when she landed it solidly.

If they liked that move, I knew they would like Britt's standing full twist, which was probably one of the most showstopping skills in the entire competition. I held my breath as she set up for it, standing straight and tall in the middle of the balance beam, both of her arms up by her ears as she bent her legs, launching herself into the back twist.

But when she landed, only one foot was actually on the beam, and she slipped and landed on the blue mat beneath. I winced, almost like it had happened to me.

"That's okay," I whispered under my breath. "It's all right. Just get back up and finish."

In a competition, if you fall on a skill, you don't have to try to repeat it, since you've already lost the points for the connection and gotten a deduction for the mistake. But Britt climbed back up on the beam, and instead of continuing on to her next series of leaps, she set herself up for the standing full twist again.

"What is she doing?" I muttered. I knew that if I fell or wobbled or had any other major error, the last thing I would have wanted was to make my routine last *longer*. Usually, it was hard not to hurry through the next few skills, because I was so anxious to get off that beam and make sure there was no other chance for a mess-up. Sometimes that rushing could actually lead to another mistake, so you had to be careful about that, too.

"Oh, my God, she's trying it again," Jessie said. None of us could help watching now. I stood up, because it made me feel less helpless, even though I knew that she was up there and I was down here and there was nothing I could do.

Britt's second attempt was definitely better—both of her feet landed on the beam this time. But her body was a little piked on the landing, which meant that her center of balance was off. She flailed, and even from this distance, I could see her toes curled around the beam, as she tried to hold on. Unfortunately, she couldn't, and she had to jump down from the beam to avoid falling on her face.

I heard Jessie gasp beside me.

"That's okay," I said, louder this time, as if Britt's meet wasn't pretty much trashed. Although you didn't have to attempt the skill again, if you did and you fell, it counted as another deduction from your score. Plus, Britt was now in danger of going over the time limit for her routine, which could result in more tenths of a point off.

"Come on, Britt!" I shouted.

"You can do it!" Noelle yelled next to me, trying to do that same funny accent that Britt did and failing miserably. I grinned at her.

Even Mo's lips twitched slightly, although her face didn't show much—whether she was disappointed, angry, or concerned. She looked the same as she had when Jessie was up on the beam and nailed it, and when Noelle was up there and knocked it out of the park.

Britt climbed back up onto the beam. I couldn't believe it when she set up for her standing back full *again*. How many times would she try it?

I almost couldn't watch, but somehow I felt like if I took my gaze off her, I would take away some of my support as well. It might have been superstitious, but right then, I couldn't chance it.

Up on the beam, Britt took a deep breath. Then she was flying backward, her knees tucked in close to her body as she twisted around once, landing back on the beam with that solid *thwack* that was the sweetest sound in the world.

"Yeah!" Jessie yelled. I reached out to squeeze

Noelle's hand. Britt was definitely one hundred percent certifiable, but she had done it. She had landed a standing back full in the biggest competition of her life.

The rest of her routine passed uneventfully, and when Britt's score came in, it confirmed what we'd feared. She got penalized for her two falls, her wobble, *and* for going over the time limit.

I glanced at Britt uncertainly. If I had gotten a score like that, I would've been totally devastated. Britt's blue eyes were uncharacteristically serious for a moment, but then they lit up again, and she held up her hands for high fives.

"Lowest score in the competition!" she said, as though it was a good thing.

We had to grab our stuff to rotate to the next event. As Britt brought up the rear, I turned around to see Mo give her a swift hug. "You make grandmother proud," she said.

We moved on to the floor, where everyone got time to warm up for the event first, running through a couple of tumbling passes before the rotation started. Watching Britt, Jessie, and Noelle flip across the blue carpet made me realize that I missed this event the most. I couldn't wait for this injury to be a thing of the past so I could get out there and twist and leap and dance with everyone else.

One Chinese girl did a double layout on floor, her body flipping like a pencil through the air. It was insane. From what I'd seen, the international girls had been just as busy as we had, adding new skills to their routines.

I felt a new motivation, stronger than I'd ever felt before. Once I was able to compete on floor again, I was going to add that double Arabian to my routine, and I was going to get so good at it that I would be able to drill it into the carpet even on my worst days. Maybe it wouldn't earn me a gold medal or a trip to the Olympics, but it would make people carch their breath for a moment, to say, *Wow, look at what that girl can do.*

Warm-up was over, and all the girls except for the next one up had to clear the podium. The first gymnast on the floor was a Romanian girl who did an amazing job until she over-rotated a double twist and stepped out of bounds. I clapped for her, because even though she was technically one of our competitors, in truth it was hard to see *anyone* fall or mess up, no matter who it was.

Luckily, Jessie made no major mistakes in her

routine, and Britt's floor music got everyone in the audience clapping along with its bouncy beat. Finally, Noelle took her place in the center of the floor, and the first strains of her *Riverdance* music started up.

Mihai had already told me that he wasn't going to be able to come to Noelle's competition, even though he'd wanted to be there ("and not *just* for my little sister," he'd said to me, which had made me blush a little). The drive to New Orleans wasn't that far, but his family would've had to close down the store, and between that and the cost of hotel rooms and stuff, I guess it was too much.

Still, I couldn't help smiling when I thought of him and the funny impressions he'd done of the Irish dancers with their stiff upper bodies and crazy kicking legs.

The dance looked much more graceful when Noelle did it in her routine, of course. She flew through all of her skills, including a two-and-a-half twist that she landed perfectly, throwing her arms up and arching her back in a salute. When she finished the routine, I could tell that her smile wasn't just for the judges.

"Awesome!" I said, hugging her when she came

down from the podium. "You were amazing up there."

After her floor score was posted, I wanted to tell her that she was less than a tenth of a point away from the lead, but I didn't want to freak her out. Mo always told us to leave our calculators at school, meaning that she didn't want us trying to figure out what score we needed or how other people were doing. Once, Britt had challenged her about that, asking what we were supposed to do if we needed a perfect ten to win but didn't know that. Mo looked her right in the eyes and said, "You do perfect ten routine whether you know or not."

I wondered what was going through Noelle's mind as we packed up our bags and moved to the last event, vault. She might not have known the exact numbers, but she had to be aware that she was having the competition of her life, and could very well take the all-around gold medal. I'd never really had that feeling before, so I didn't know what it would be like. Would it motivate you, push you further, or would it overwhelm you and make you nervous?

Mo must've been having similar thoughts, because once we put our bags down on the sidelines, she squeezed Noelle's shoulder, although when she spoke, it was to all of us. She glanced from Britt to Jessie to Noelle and finally to me, although I obviously wasn't going to be competing on this event.

"Do your best," she said. "You have had good meet, and now there is one more. So, do your best."

Britt and Noelle did the exact same vault: a Yurchenko one-and-a-half twist. Britt's looked like most of hers did in practice, with a ton of height and distance but a huge hop forward on the landing. Britt's problem on vault was that she didn't always know how to control it, which meant that she sometimes over-rotated her twists a little bit or had trouble keeping her feet in one place on the mat. It probably wouldn't be long before Cheng had her doing a Yurchenko double or two-and-a-half, because if she had too much power on her vault right now, it might actually help to give her more flips and twists to make use of that power.

I had the opposite problem with my vaults. I only did a Yurchenko full—a half twist less than Noelle's and Britt's vault—and already I had issues pushing off the table with my hands to get enough height to complete all my rotations. But maybe that was another good effect of my injury, if I wanted to see the silver lining of it: I was more inspired than ever to get back in the gym and work on all that stuff I hadn't been able to do for the past two months.

The girl who was currently in the lead went before Noelle, and although she did a decent vault, she took a couple of steps on her landing. When her score flashed up on the screen, I knew Noelle had a chance at catching up to her. But Noelle, who was standing on the podium waiting for the judges to tell her to go, might still have had no idea.

Even Jessie was watching Noelle, although she was next up on the vault and should have been stretching and preparing. We couldn't help it. Britt glanced at the scoreboard, and said, "Could she—"

I nodded before she finished. I knew exactly what she was going to ask, and it was true. Noelle *could* win. She needed just one vault to do it.

Mo was staring at the floor, and for a second I was, like, *Are you crazy? You're not even going to watch her?* But then she glanced up again, and I realized that she'd been saying something to herself in Chinese under her breath, almost like a prayer. I'd never seen her do anything like that in a competition before. It made this moment even more intense. We all waited to see what Noelle would do.

Noelle saluted the judges and took her place on

the vault runway. We all had our preferences as to where we liked to start on the long strip of blue carpet, which we would mark with a line of white chalk before the rotation started. Noelle looked graceful even while taking her place, pointing her toes as she aligned herself with her mark.

She took a deep breath, and then she was running, her fists pumping at her sides while she hurtled toward the vault, launching into a round-off so that she was facing backward as her feet hit the springboard. She bent back until her hands touched the vaulting table, and with one strong shove, she was in the air, flipping and twisting.

Now it was our turn to take deep breaths. Beside me, Britt was biting her nails.

Noelle drilled her feet into the mat, not moving them a single inch as she threw her hands up in a salute. She was grinning as she jumped down from the podium, her usual serious competition face totally gone. We all enveloped her in a group hug, cheering and congratulating her even though they hadn't posted her score yet.

"Girls," Mo said, trying to warn us. It was true that we shouldn't have been getting ahead of ourselves, since there was always the possibility that the judges would find some slight thing to penalize her for and she wouldn't score the extra tenth of a point she needed to take the lead. But we didn't care.

That slim possibility was definitely on Noelle's mind, though, since while we kept congratulating her and telling her how awesome she was, she only asked, "What's my score? Did they post it?"

Jessie was supposed to be up on the podium by now, ready to take her turn on the vault, but she waited with all of us through the eternity it seemed to take for Noelle's score to show on the board. It was like it happened in slow motion. Suddenly, the LED screen flashed 9.85, and Noelle's name moved above that of the Ukrainian gymnast who had been in first place. The crowd went wild. Then *we* went wild.

"You did it!" we shouted, jumping around her like we'd binged on energy drinks before the competition. "You did it!"

She smiled, a happy but slightly overwhelmed look in her eyes. "*We* did it," she said. "We did it."

Thirteen

Mo had told us we'd have a strict lights-out policy of nine o'clock, to make sure we got enough rest the night before the final day of competition. On the one hand, I was totally exhausted. Even though I hadn't competed on as many events as my teammates, I was feeling like my mental and emotional energy had been drained by being on the edge of my seat the whole competition.

On the other hand, all I wanted to do was stay up forever and relive every moment. We were all sitting on Noelle's bed—she and I were sharing a room, with Jessie and Britt in the other room in the suite—admiring her gold medal.

"It looks so *real*," Jessie said.

"It's not real gold," Britt pointed out. "It's basically a bunch of other metals covered in gold foil."

I glared at her, and she threw up her hands. "It's very *nice* gold foil," she said. "I'm not talking aluminum wrap here. And it's still the coolest thing I've ever seen in my life. I'm just *saying*."

Jessie gave her a playful slap on the leg. "That wasn't what I meant, anyway. It looks so official, I guess."

We'd all won medals before, and Britt and Noelle and I had even won them in an Elite competition. Noelle already had a gold medal, but it was for her work on the beam. It wasn't anything to sneer at—being the national champion on the balance beam—but being the Junior American Invitational all-around champion definitely had a ring to it.

"Do you think there can be a four-way tie at the Olympics?" Britt asked. "Like, what if we planned all our routines to be the exact same difficulty level, and then we made the exact same mistakes, and then—"

"Wait, why do we have to make mistakes?" I asked.

Britt absently twirled the end of her ponytail. "If we're talking about me, there will have to be some mistakes."

I touched Noelle's medal again. It had a groove running along the outside rim that was the perfect size for my finger. I traced its circular shape. It had been hard to accept that I had never been in the running for this medal, but it had also been kind of nice to be able to root for my teammates without thinking like a competitor. I wondered if that was closer to the way it felt to be on a college team. Even though you were still vying for individual medals, you wore your school's colors and represented a unified front against all the other schools. It might be kind of fun.

Mo knocked on the door before poking her head in. "Jessie and Britt, you need to be in own room," she said. "Light out in ten minute."

Britt bounced off the bed, while Jessie gave Noelle and me a hug. "Catch you on the flip side," Britt said. "Get it?"

I rolled my eyes. "Of course we get it," I said. "You've made that pun before."

Britt only smiled, blowing us a jaunty kiss before she and Jessie left to go to their room. Our suite was really nice, with an eat-in kitchen where Mo had made us a healthy breakfast that morning. For tomorrow, she had promised us scrambled eggs, which Britt would load up with ketchup like she always did.

Mo slept in the living room, on a foldout couch. She said she didn't mind doing that, so that we could each have beds of our own and get some good rest for the competition, but I also think she did it so that she could keep an eye on us.

After dinner that night, my mom had given me a really nice, long hug.

"What's that for?" I'd asked her.

"I'm so proud of you," she'd said. Her eyes had been oddly sparkly, almost like she was about to cry.

"*Mom,*" I'd said, kind of embarrassed. "All I did was qualify for the bars final. Noelle's the one who got a medal today."

"Yes," my mother had said, "but you were breathtaking."

I'd never heard myself or my gymnastics described that way before, but I liked it. Now, after Noelle and I changed into our pajamas and brushed our teeth and we were lying in the dark waiting for

Mo to check on us, I turned the word over and over in my head. *Breathtaking*.

"Noelle?" I said.

I could hear her rustling the sheets, like she was rolling over to face me. "Yeah?"

"Do you feel any different?" I asked. "Now that you've won the all-around, I mean? Do you feel like, more special?"

She was silent for so long that I almost prompted her again, thinking maybe she'd fallen asleep, but then I heard her sigh. "It feels amazing," she said. "Knowing I worked so hard for it, and now I can always say that I was the first American Invitational Junior champion ever. . . . Yeah, it's pretty great. But I know that Monday, we'll be in the gym, and I'll be doing vault timers and beam reps like any other week. So I guess it feels special now, and I'm just trying to enjoy it before it's back to the same old routine."

The best medal I'd won so far had been a bronze on the bars in the National Championships, but I understood what she meant. I'd glowed about that achievement for weeks, sneaking up to my room to look at the shiny bronze medal before school and after dinner and any other time I could. But eventually the medal started feeling like one more thing on my walls, like the framed artwork my mother had put up of a famous artist's ballet dancers.

I thought of that word my mother had used—*breathtaking*—and the way her face had looked when she said it. Somehow, I couldn't foresee that losing its sparkle anytime soon. Instead of leaving it on my walls to be forgotten, I planned to carry it with me always.

The next day, it was my turn to compete again in the event finals for the bars. Noelle had also qualified, and she went second in the rotation. I knew she'd done a good job when I heard the applause she got when she landed her dismount, but I didn't watch her. I was too nervous.

Then they signaled to me that I could take my place on the podium, to wait for my chance to go. The Chinese girl who'd gone after Noelle was still swinging around the bars, but I stood at the chalk bowl and reapplied chalk to my hands, trying to breathe deeply in and out without choking on the bits of white powder floating in the air.

As I stood there, for some reason everything

started to hit me at once. I was very aware of the fact that, in under two minutes, every single person in the arena would be watching me up on the bars. There were huge lights, and I was wearing a sparkly red leotard with a silver line across the chest like a wave. My teammates were on the sidelines, waiting to call out my name as soon as it was my turn to go, and my parents were in the stands, my mother probably gripping my father's hand as her stomach turned over just like mine was doing now.

I was psyching myself out, so I tried to think about something else, anything that would make me forget about the pressure and the attention and focus on my gymnastics. And weirdly, the only thing I could come up with was the essay I'd written for Ms. Rine. After she'd given it back to me with a big A+ written on the top in red pen and gushing comments throughout, I'd read it over and over, wanting to savor one of the first school assignments I'd ever been truly proud of.

Christina Flores Five Years From Now:

When I think about myself in five years, I know that above everything else, I want to be happy. I'm a gymnast, and I have high expectations for myself. Other people have high expectations for me, too—like my mom, who always reminds me of how much work we've both put into this dream, and how important it is that I don't blow it. My coach, Mo, also wants me to be one of the best gymnasts in the world.

The Chinese gymnast dismounted to loud applause. It was louder than the applause for Noelle, if I had to judge honestly, and now I knew that she was the girl to beat. I wiped some excess chalk on my thighs, and waited for the judges to wave the green flag telling me I could mount the bars.

Right now, it's hard to be happy sometimes, because I feel like so many people are depending on me. They believe in me, and that makes me feel like I can fly, but they also are counting on me to do my best, and that makes me worried that I'll fall. In five years, I hope to have figured out how to juggle these two things, so that I can live up to my potential but not worry so much about what everyone else thinks.

The head judge raised the green flag. I took a deep breath and saluted, raising both my arms in the air and arching my back; then I faced the bars.

In Dickens's novel, Pip has "great" expectations, but I've always been taught that "great" is a vague word that doesn't mean much. Maybe that's part of my problem. I want to be great, but I don't know what that means. Do I have to win an Olympic medal? Because I don't know if I can. What if I win an NCAA National Championship instead, or what if I don't win anything at all, but compete on a college team? What if I study art and just try to figure out if I am any good at something besides gymnastics? What does it even mean to be "good," much less great?

My feet barely skimmed over the mat as I grabbed the bar and swung into my mount. I used the kip to pull myself up into a handstand, which I held for a few seconds, knowing that the judges wanted to see precision in those kinds of moves. By the time I transitioned up to the high bar, I was feeling confident. Everything just felt right. My body was like an arrow, knowing exactly how to pierce the air to hit its target.

Happiness is important to me because it has to come from within. It can't be given to me by my parents under the Christmas tree, or by my coach in her praise, or even by my teacher in a grade. It has to come from me, and the way I feel about myself.

I was getting set for my big release combination, making sure I was centered over the bar in order to catch the Tkachev correctly. Everything hinged on that first release, because if I caught it wrong, I would have to bail on the second skill, and since I wouldn't have enough time to make that decision, I would probably fall on the Gienger. But when my hands left the bar, I somehow knew. It was perfect. I straddled my legs, catching the bar again easily and swinging forward only to let go once more for the Gienger. There was no way to describe the amazing security and relief that came over me when I felt that parchmentlike texture of the bar beneath my hands again and knew I'd nailed it.

So, in five years, my biggest expectation for myself is that I will be happy, and that I'll have learned how to take everyone's support and encouragement but will also remember to look within for my own self-worth. Although, really, what am I waiting for? I should expect that from myself now. In my eyes, that would be true greatness.

I couldn't allow myself to relax, though, because I still had my dismount to finish the routine. I hadn't practiced my full-twisting double tuck that much, in order to take it easy on my Achilles injury. So as I swung faster and faster around the bar, building speed for my dismount, it was hard not to think, *Don't mess up, don't mess up.* But I forced myself to stop thinking.

I let go of the bar and let go of all my doubts at the same time. It was too late now for any second-guessing. I was in the air, twisting and flipping. It felt like it was milliseconds and yet eons before my feet hit the mat. My body pitched forward a bit, but I willed my feet to stick to that mat. Once I'd recovered, I threw my hands up in the air, and I didn't even have to fake a smile for the judges.

My teammates were waiting for me when I got off the podium. I jumped down to give them all a huge hug. Even Mo joined in, making it a group hug with the whole team. I was so busy laughing with them and enjoying the energy vibrating through my body that I almost forgot to be worried about my score.

Almost. But then I heard Noelle gasp next to me, and I knew they'd posted the number up on the display. I turned and saw it, lit up in bright lights.

It was a 9.8. One of the highest scores I'd ever earned on bars, but still not enough to beat the Chinese gymnast who went before me. Out of the corner of my eye, I saw her teammates congratulating her, exchanging high fives.

"I'm sorry," Noelle said, rubbing my back. She'd finished fourth on bars, but she already had her all-around gold, and another chance at a medal on beam coming up next.

"You know what?" I said. "I just won a silver medal. I won a silver medal!"

I hugged my teammates again, letting out a whoop of excitement. I couldn't be disappointed with myself; I'd done my best out there, and even though I'd only competed on one event, I'd proven that I was a good gymnast.

Or maybe "good" was selling myself short. I was Aurelia Christina Flores, the first Mexican American Junior Elite to win a silver medal at the American Invitational, and I was great.

Gymnastics glossary

all-around competition: The part of a competition where gymnasts compete in all four events, and in which their combined scores are used to determine who is the best all-around athlete

Arabian: A skill where the gymnast jumps backward, as though to perform a backflip, but does a half twist in the air to complete a front flip and lands facing forward

beam: A horizontal, raised apparatus that is four inches wide, sixteen feet in length, and approximately four feet off the floor; on this, gymnasts perform a series of dance moves and acrobatic skills.

blind landing: A landing in which the gymnast ends up facing forward, sometimes away from the apparatus, and she cannot see the floor before landing

event finals: The part of a competition in which the gymnasts with the highest preliminary scores from one event compete to determine who the best gymnast is on that apparatus

floor: A carpeted surface measuring forty feet square, over springs and wooden boards. Also the term for the only event in which a gymnast performs a routine set to music; the routine is ninety seconds in length, and composed of dance and acrobatic elements.

full-in: Two flips in the air with the first flip featuring a 360-degree twist

Gienger: A release skill performed on the uneven bars, in which the gymnast swings upward and releases the bar to perform a backflip with a half turn before catching the bar again

handspring: A move in which a gymnast starts on both feet, jumps to a position supporting her body with just her two hands on the floor, and then pushes off to land on her feet again. This can be done forward or backward, and is typically used to start or connect an acrobatic series.

Junior Elite: The level before Senior Elite, as designated by regulations of the governing body of gymnastics. Junior Elite gymnasts are not allowed to compete in the Olympics.

kip: A basic skill performed on the uneven bars that requires a lot of upper-body strength and is often used as a mount. In a kip, the gymnast points her toes and brings her feet toward the upper bar, piking her body to pull herself into a position on the lower bar in which her arms are straight and her thighs rest against the bar.

layout: A maneuver completed in the air with hands held against the body and a pencil-straight overall position; flipping can be forward or backward, and the move ends with the gymnast standing on both feet again.

Pak salto: A release skill used on the bars to transition from the high bar to the low bar, in which the gymnast swings forward on the high bar toward the low bar, lets go to complete one full backflip, and then catches the low bar, while passing through a handstand position

pike: A position in which the body is bent double at the hips, with legs straight and toes pointed

plié: A ballet movement that involves a low squat, with the back completely straight

press handstand: A move beginning on the floor with legs in a straddle position and all of the weight on the hands. The entire body is raised over the head and moves from a straddle position into a straight-body handstand.

release skill: Any skill performed on the uneven bars that requires the gymnast's hands to leave the bar before returning to it, usually after a twisting or flipping skill has been executed

ring leap: A leap in which one of the gymnast's legs is stretched out in front of her, and the other bent behind her, with her toes touching the back of her head

round-off: A move that begins like a cartwheel, but in which the legs swing together overhead, and the gymnast finishes facing in the opposite direction

sheep jump: A move in which the gymnast jumps into the air, throws her head back until it touches her feet for a split second, and then returns to a straight-body position to land on both feet

standing full twist: A move that begins in a stationary position on both feet, followed by a jump into a flip with a 360-degree twist in the air (usually in a tucked position with legs bent at a ninety-degree angle) before a landing on both feet. Typically, this move is completed on floor or beam.

tuck: A position in which the knees are folded in toward the chest at a ninety-degree angle, with the waist bent, creating the shape of a ball

tumbling passes: A series of connected acrobatic moves required in a floor-exercise routine

turnout: The basis of many ballet skills, it is the rotation of the leg and foot out from the center of the body, and is an exhibition of great extension and grace for the dancer.

Tkachev: Sometimes referred to as a *reverse hecht*, this release skill, performed on the uneven bars, involves the gymnast's swinging forward from a handstand, then flying backward over the bar and catching it again. This skill is named for the Soviet gymnast Alexander Tkachev.

twist: A rotation of the body around the horizontal and vertical axes. Twisting is completed when a gymnast is flipping simultaneously, performing both actions at the same time in the same element. Twisting elements are typically named for the number of rotations completed (e.g.: a half twist is 180 degrees, or half a rotation; a full twist is 360 degrees, or a full rotation; and a double twist is 720 degrees, or two complete rotations).

uneven bars: (often, just "bars") one of four apparatuses in women's artistic gymnastics. Bars features the apparatus on which women perform mostly using their upper-body strength. This event consists of two rails placed at an uneven level; one bar acts as the high bar and the other as the low bar. Both bars are flexible, helping the gymnast to connect skills from one to the other.